To the chocolate egg hidden away in the garden of our old house during an Easter Egg hunt, I hope someone finds you eventually!

THE O'MALLEY & SWIFT CRIME THRILLERS

Corn Dolls
Foxton Girls
We All Fall Down
The House of Secrets
The Uninvited Guest
Deadly Games
One Last Breath
Still Waters
Vanishing Act
Chill Pill
Bleeding Hearts
The Ghost Portrait
Escape Room

THE GHOST PORTRAIT

Copyright © 2025 by K.T. Galloway

Published worldwide by A.W.E. Publishing.

This edition published in 2025

Copyright © 2025 by K.T. Galloway. The right of K.T. Galloway to be identified as the author of this work has been asserted in accordance with the Copyright, Design and Patents Act 1988.

All rights reserved. No part of this book may be reproduced in any form or by any electronic or mechanical means, including information storage and retrieval systems, without written permission from the author, except for the use of brief quotations in a book review.

All characters and events in this book are entirely fictional. Any references to historical events, real people, or real locales are used fictitiously. Other names, characters, places, and incidents are the product of the author's imagination, and any resemblance to actual events or locales or persons, living or dead, is entirely coincidental.

Cover design by Kate Smith

Edited by GS & LW

THE GHOST PORTRAIT

AN O'MALLEY & SWIFT NOVEL
BOOK 12

K.T. GALLOWAY

Every Masterpiece Hides a Secret

When renowned artist Eliza Warren is found dead in her studio, there's no sign of violence. But her expression is one of pure terror. Annie O'Malley & DI Joe Swift have seen a lot of crime scenes, but nothing like this. Eliza wasn't just killed—she was frightened to death.

At the centre of the studio sits an unfinished portrait, its subject haunting. But when Annie starts asking questions, the painting vanishes and the case takes a darker turn.

The woman in the portrait is linked to an unsolved disappearance from twenty years ago—that of Margot Grayson, who was last seen in the orbit of powerful art collector Edward Brannon.

As Annie and Swift dig deeper, they realise someone is determined to keep Margot's story buried. Witnesses are silenced. The past is rewritten. And then, another body appears—posed like a work of art.

Somewhere in Eliza's stolen painting lies the truth. A truth someone is willing to kill for.

Can O'Malley and Swift find the ghost portrait and find Eliza's killer before one of their team becomes the next macabre exhibition?

MAILING LIST

Thank you for reading THE GHOST PORTRAIT
(O'Malley & Swift Book Twelve)

While you're here, why not sign-up to my readers' club where you be the first to hear my news, enter competitions, and read exclusive content:

[**Join KT Galloway's Reader Club**](#)
at ktgallowaybooks.com

FOREWORD

Well, here we are—Book 12!

I can hardly believe it myself. Thank you so much for sticking with me on this journey, and for staying by Annie and Swift's side through every case, every late-night lead, and every moment of chaos. It means the world to know you're still here.

This time, we take a little trip into the murky corners of the art world (which I'm fairly sure—*hopefully*—is nothing like the real art world!)

As always, the setting is Norfolk, but the towns, streets, and cafés etc are all entirely made up.

I really hope you enjoy this twisty, eerie case—and thank you, as ever, for reading.

Enjoy 😊

PROLOGUE

The studio was quiet, save for the faint hum of the electric heater battling against the chill seeping through the old brick walls. Eliza Warren rubbed her hands together, the sharp sting of the cold making her joints ache and her skin prickle. Despite the light from the overhead spots, the room felt shadowed; the night itself had crept inside and nestled in the corners of the studio amongst the blank canvasses and the ones Eliza had painted then discarded.

These canvases were arranged like sentinels along the walls, some draped in protective sheets, others bare and raw. Each one was a tiny fragment of her life's work, yet none quite as unsettling as the painting that now balanced on the spare easel in the corner by the window.

Her unfinished portrait.

She avoided looking directly at it as she worked on other pieces, adjusting the placement of smaller pieces destined for her latest exhibition. She'd painted hundreds of portraits over the years—faces of strangers, loved ones, even herself—but this one was different. It had been from the start.

The subject was a woman. A face that had haunted her dreams for months, years even. She'd woken in a cold sweat one night, the image of those piercing grey eyes burned into her mind. Throwing the cat from the blankets, Eliza had rushed down the stairs to her studio before the vision faded and had painted with the ferocity of an axe murderer going at his prey. The paint had covered her and dotted the concrete floor, but she'd had tunnel vision. Unable to look away from her work until the first new layer had been put to canvas.

Now, the portrait just rested on the easel, accusing and incomplete.

Eliza set down the brush she'd been holding and wiped her hands on her apron. The studio felt colder than it should have, even with the heater running. She turned her head, drawn by the faintest tug of awareness, her gaze landing on the painting.

The woman's unfinished face seemed to glow in the light, her pale features almost luminescent against the shadowy background. Her lips were parted slightly, as if about to speak, and her eyes—those eyes—seemed alive, full of a quiet rage that Eliza could feel in her chest.

She shivered and turned away.

"It's just a painting," she muttered under her breath, forcing herself to focus on the tasks at hand.

Her final exhibition. That was how the gallery director had described it, though Eliza hadn't thought of it in such dramatic terms. It wasn't as though she was hanging up her paint brushes, just that these days she found her hands weren't quite as willing as they had been, and her eyesight wasn't quite as sharp as it once was. Still, there was a weight to the planned event. After decades of perfecting her craft, of creating images that seemed to breathe and pulse with life, Eliza felt a deep sadness at the director's counsel.

She reached for a small canvas leaning against the wall, its gilded frame catching the light, but her hands trembled as she lifted it.

Behind her, the air seemed to shift.

She froze, the canvas slipping slightly in her grip. The studio was empty—she knew that. The door was locked, the windows bolted shut. But there it was again, that sensation, like the wisp of a hand against her shoulder.

"Eliza," she whispered to herself. "You're overworked. Tired. Getting older. That's all."

But even as she said it, she couldn't ignore the creeping unease. Slowly, she turned her head, her gaze flicking back to the unfinished portrait.

Her breath caught in her throat.

Something was different.

The woman's face hadn't changed—at least, not at

first glance. But there was something in her expression, a subtle shift that Eliza couldn't quite place. Her lips seemed tighter, almost curling into the faintest of smiles.

Eliza took a step closer, her heartbeat thundering in her ears.

"It's just the light," she said aloud, her voice reedy.

She reached out to adjust the lamp above the easel, hoping a change in angle would banish the illusion. The light flickered briefly before settling, casting stark shadows across the woman's face.

Her grey eyes were watching Eliza. Knowingly.

Eliza stumbled back, her hip colliding with a low table and sending a jar of brushes clattering to the floor. She gasped, the sound sharp in the thick silence it had broken. The painting hadn't moved. It *couldn't* have moved.

And yet.

The longer she stared, the more convinced she became that the woman's expression had shifted again. Her lips were no longer parted, and her eyes—those impossibly vivid eyes—seemed to glisten with tears.

"No," Eliza whispered, shaking her head. "This isn't real. I'm imagining it."

But her gaze was fixed on the canvas, unable to look away. The air in the studio felt heavy, as charged as the sky moments before the crack of a thunderstorm. She could hear her own breathing, shallow and quick, playing a sorry tune against the ticking of the old clock on the windowsill.

And then it happened.

A movement.

Not in the studio, but on the canvas. The woman's head tilted ever so slightly, her eyes narrowing as if she were focusing on Eliza.

Eliza screamed, stumbling back again and nearly tripping over the scattered brushes. Her back hit the wall, and she pressed herself against it, her hands trembling as they gripped the fabric of her painting apron.

The lights flickered once more, casting the studio into brief, suffocating darkness before flaring back to life.

The painting was no longer serene.

The woman's face an expression, twisted into something cruel, her mouth curling into a sneer that stretched unnaturally wide. Her eyes, the very reason Eliza had fought to paint this portrait, now black pits, endless and hollow.

"Eliza," a voice whispered, low and rasping, from somewhere deep within the room.

Eliza's heart stopped. The sound wasn't human, it was a voice carried on the wind. She scanned the room frantically, but there was no one there.

"No," she said, her voice trembling. "This isn't happening."

The shadows in the studio seemed to thicken, pooling from the corners and stretching toward her like grasping hands. The light flickered again, plunging the room into darkness for longer this time.

When the light returned, the painting was different again.

The woman was gone.

The canvas was blank, the brushstrokes of the background smeared as if someone had dragged a hand across the wet paint.

Eliza's knees buckled, and she sank to the floor, her breath coming in shallow gasps. She stared at the empty canvas, her mind racing to make sense of what she had seen.

Then, slowly, she turned her head toward the corner of the room.

And there she was.

The woman from the painting stood in the shadows, her pale face illuminated by the faint glow of the heater. She stepped forward, her bare feet soundless against the wooden floor.

Eliza tried to scream, but no sound came.

The last thing she saw before the light flickered and died a final death, was the woman's terrifying face, inches from her own.

ONE

SUNDAY

The late morning sun spilled through the windows of DI Joe Swift's kitchen, casting a warm glow over the chaos unfolding at the island. Annie O'Malley, perched on the edge of a stool, surveying the scene, a single brow raised. A dozen brightly coloured, foil wrapped, chocolate eggs were scattered across the marble alongside stacks of tiny chocolate bunnies, an indecipherable hand-drawn map, and a mound of shredded pastel tissue paper.

"This," Annie said, holding up a neon-pink egg, "is a disaster waiting to happen."

Swift glanced up from where he was furiously scribbling onto a pad of paper. He was still in his joggers, his hair damp from a rushed shower, looking pretty cute, Annie thought.

"It's not a disaster," he said slowly, though there was a faint edge of panic in his voice. "It's... er, organised chaos."

Annie laughed. "How long have we got before everyone arrives? We still need to bake the cake, sort out the sandwiches, put out the fluffy chicks in the garden, and hide all these eggs in their secret locations. And, I hate to say it, but your map looks like it was drawn by a drunk spider. On rollerskates."

Swift frowned at the map, tilting it as if that might improve its legibility. "It's a symbolic representation."

"Of what, your mind?" Annie grinned as she grabbed a thick marker pen and a fresh sheet of paper. "Here, let me fix it. You're better at solving murders than you are at planning Easter egg hunts, and that's saying something."

Swift gave her a pointed look but didn't argue. He sat back on his stool, arms crossed, and watched as Annie began sketching a much neater map of his sprawling back garden to give to the guests arriving in less than an hour. Annie didn't actually think the other members of their team would mind about the egg hunt, as long as they got their fill of chocolate. DS Belle Lock, otherwise known as Tink for her small stature and fierce nature, and DS Tom Page made up the rest of the Major Crime Unit, or MCU. And, along with their boss, DCI Hannah Robins, they were heading over for an afternoon of Easter fun. But it was the peripheral team members who Annie was worried about. The ones who they didn't spend a lot of time with, the ones who were bringing their kids. And kids could be brutal when there was organised fun and chocolate involved.

The garden Annie was sketching, much like the rest of Swift's home, was huge. It stretched back almost half an acre. But, while the house was immaculate in its Victorian gothic, turreted splendour, the garden was filled with overgrown bushes, a pond with a weed problem, and a corner that may have at one time been a rockery. Annie had jokingly dubbed it 'the wilderness' but she loved everything about it. Just as she loved everything about Joe Swift.

Almost everything. She wasn't too keen on his organisational skills right at that moment.

"Remind me why we're doing this again?" she asked, chewing the end of the marker thoughtfully as she tried to work out how to draw the large willow tree that took up the other back corner of the garden.

"Team morale," Swift said. "The MCU's been worked to the bone these last few months. Double shifts, high-profile cases. People need a break and a bit of fun once in a while."

He wasn't wrong. Since Annie had joined the team, a little over two years ago now, they had been run ragged with the weird and the wonderful crimes that the other teams weren't able to deal with. Anything from plague doctors to a swimming pool full of bodies whose hearts had been taken as an aperitif by a man who thought they'd help him be a better person. Not a case went by where Annie didn't use her training as a psychotherapist to get into the minds of criminals she'd rather not. Still, she wouldn't have it any other way.

"True that, I'm sure everyone will love an outing away from the whiteboards and incident rooms. I'm still shocked that you're opening your home up to them though. Tink and Page, yes, but the rest of the squad, that's some good bossing there."

Swift's expression softened, a hint of a smile tugging at the corner of his mouth. "You're the one who said we should do something here because it would be cheaper than hiring out a hall."

"Whoopsie, did I?" Annie said, pointing the marker at him. "That was a crazy suggestion of mine. Ignore me next time. Let's go zorbing, or paint balling, or to an escape room or something like that."

"It'll be fine," Swift said, leaning forward to inspect her work. "What's that squiggle?"

"The pond. You need to put a clear warning near it, unless you want someone's kid falling in."

Swift raised an eyebrow. "We could push Tink in?"

"No, Tink is one of the good ones." Annie laughed. Tink and Swift were like brother and sister, always squabbling, but when they put their heads together, they were second to none. Annie loved her team; she was thankful every day that she was scooped up and welcomed into the fold right when she needed a family who weren't biological.

"Fair enough, what about Charlie, last week I saw him tip his tea dregs into the office plant."

Annie almost choked on the mini eggs she'd been sampling. "If I remember correctly, Swift, you did that not long ago yourself. How is the plant, by the way?"

"Still upstairs, growing like a weed now though. And its secret replacement had been doing well until Charlie drowned it in Earl Grey. If anyone inspects it too much, they'll know it's not the original and I'll be found out."

"And by anyone, you mean Tink?"

Swift nodded, grimacing.

"Let's hope that Fiddle Leaves like tea then, and not the hideous stuff you'd been forced to drink when you tipped it away into Tink's office pride and joy."

They both looked down at the completed map and contemplated what they were doing with their lives.

"Here you go." Annie pushed the map in Swift's direction. "There. A masterpiece worthy of framing. Once the guests have decimated the goods, of course."

Swift studied it for a moment, then nodded. "Not bad."

"Not bad?" Annie echoed, mock offended. "It's brilliant, and you know it."

Swift chuckled, setting the map aside. "Fine. It's brilliant. Now, let's get these eggs hidden before everyone starts arriving."

"Off you go," Annie said, waving him away with the bag full of foil wrapped eggs. "There's still sandwiches to prep and a cake to bake, not to mention…"

Joe held a finger up and Annie stopped talking.

"Let's not mention then, yeah?" He laughed,

ducking out the room as Annie threw a balled-up Creme Egg wrapper in his direction. "Come find me in ten if I'm not back. I may have been swallowed by the Creature from the Black Lagoon that I'm sure now lives in my pond."

Annie laughed to herself as she set about making the batter for a chocolate cake. Her trusty Nigella cookbook fell open at the correct page because it was the only recipe Annie ever made. And flour and chocolate powder had given the spread a dusty feel, like an old painting. She loved baking in Swift's kitchen, the space was about ten times the size of her own and she had a proper range cooker here, rather than the countertop microwave. Still, her office-cum-flat in the centre of the city did her well. It was cosy and welcoming and had a pizza place underneath it. Swift had hinted a few times that she and Sunday the cat might as well make use of the space he had and move in, but family drama and decades of having to fend for herself meant that Annie wasn't quite there yet.

She bent to put the laden cake tins in one of the ovens when Swift appeared back in the kitchen.

"Did you hide them in the places we put on the map, or did you get to the back door and throw and hope for the best?" Annie asked, curling an arm around his waist and pulling him in for a kiss.

Before Swift could respond, the sound of tyres crunching on gravel echoed through the open kitchen window.

"They're on time," Swift muttered, peering over Annie's shoulder.

Annie glanced back and saw a bright yellow Punto pulling into the driveway, and two familiar figures emerged. Tink and Page both balanced a plate of snacks and a cardboard box of drink.

"Awesome," Annie said, giving Swift a peck on the cheek and unwrapping herself from his hug. "I hope it's alcoholic."

"It's Tink," Swift replied, heading for the door. "Of course it's alcoholic."

Within minutes, the kitchen was filled with laughter and chatter.

"Where's the chocolate?" Tink demanded, already rifling through Swift's cupboards.

"It's hidden in the garden," Annie said. "And you lot will be able to go hunt for it once everyone has arrived. We've got a map and everything. You're going to love it. But you have to let the kids find some, Tink."

Tink clapped her hands in glee while Page helped himself to a bunch of grapes from Swift's fruit bowl. Page was built like he spent all his spare time in the gym, but Annie knew he barely had any spare time between work and looking after his Gran, so it must have just been good genes.

"We're leaving the car here, by the way," Tink said, cracking open a can of pre-made cocktails she lifted from her carrier.

"We've got work in the morning," Swift reminded her, eyeing the can. "Plus, it's not even midday yet."

Tink held a finger up to her lips. "You get to boss me around all week; it's a Sunday, shhhh."

She took a swig, sighing happily. Annie remembered what it was like to be in her twenties and the idea of a hangover was a slightly sore head and a croaky voice. These days she needed forty-eight hours in bed with the curtains closed and no noise. And she was only thirty-seven.

Swift laughed and offered Page a beer, popping the top from a bottle for each of them. Annie helped herself to a San Pellegrino and raised her can in a toast.

"Before Traffic get here and spoil the mood," she joked. "Here's to us, the best team going."

They all cheered and took a drink, choking on their beverages as Robins cleared her throat in the doorway.

"Don't mind me," she said, though she was smiling.

Somewhere in her fifties, DCI Hannah Robins was an intimidating figure in her suits cut so well there was no way they were off the shelf. Her immaculate blonde hair sat in loose waves on her shoulders and, as ever, her lips were painted in a lipstick that Annie thought was maybe tattooed on, it was so neat.

"Guv," Swift cried, ushering her into the kitchen. "Come in, come in. What can we get you to drink? The others are due soon and then we can start the

Easter Egg hunt, and Annie's been baking a cake which will be ready shortly too. She's made the best sand…"

Robins held up a hand, cutting Swift short. Annie chuckled behind her drink, she wasn't used to seeing Swift nervously chatter like that. Maybe inviting everyone over to his house wasn't the best idea she'd ever had. Poor Swift. She blew him a sneaky kiss across the kitchen.

"Sorry," Robins said, dropping her hand. Her expression didn't shout excitement about being at an Easter Egg hunt. "I'm afraid party time is over. I've let the other teams know it's cancelled."

Tink squeaked. "But I haven't had any chocolate yet. And they've drawn a map."

Annie felt a flicker of unease as Robins shook her head and pulled out an island stool to perch on. The DCI's expression darkened further, her posture stiffening.

"What's wrong?" Annie asked.

Swift hesitated, glancing at the team. "We've got a case?"

Robins nodded.

"And no-one else can take it?" Annie probed, the smell of her cake starting to permeate the air as it baked.

The room was so still Annie could hear the fridge mechanisms whirring.

"Eliza Warren. She's been found dead in her studio," Robins started.

Annie's heart sank. "The artist?"

Robins nodded again.

"And this is a case for the MCU, why?" Swift asked.

The MCU were used to taking cases that the other teams couldn't, so Annie knew it would be something unusual.

"Unclear so far," Robins replied. "Eliza's assistant found her this morning; she thought at first it had been an accident. That Eliza had tripped and fallen over a pot of brushes. She was older, losing her eyesight, balance not what it was."

"Sounds like a case for CID." Annie walked to the range and grabbed the oven gloves, pulling out the two cakes and setting them on the marble counter top to cool.

"Evans is there already." Robins' attention was momentarily broken by the smell of the cake but she soon found it again. "He said that it wasn't an accident. He thinks that Eliza was scared to death."

TWO

THE DRIVE TO ELIZA WARREN'S STUDIO WAS QUIET. Annie stared out of the passenger window as the streets of the city blurred past, her thoughts racing. They'd spent the morning baking and hiding eggs, and now they were heading to the scene of a death. The shift in tone felt jarring, but Annie had learned to roll with it, life had a way of flipping the script when you least expected it.

"Anything I should know before we get there?" she asked, breaking the silence.

Robins had given Swift a debrief as Annie had turned off all the appliances and switched off the lights. Tink had watched forlornly as Annie had pulled the doors to the garden closed and flicked their latches. She hoped that this would be an in-and-out case and the MCU could head back to the garden and devour the chocolate. That's if the wildlife didn't get there first. Was chocolate dangerous to animals other than dogs? She hoped not, the last thing she wanted was to come back to a gruesome garden death scene of their own making.

Swift gripped the steering wheel. "Not much yet. Eliza was found in her studio by her assistant when she came to drop off some supplies. Initial call came in as a suspicious death. The first uniform on the scene said it didn't look like an accident, so it was taped off, CSI went in, CID took it to start with. Then Evans arrived and the rest is history."

"How does Evans know someone has been frightened to death without doing an autopsy first?" Annie asked, holding on to the handle above her head as Swift took a roundabout and zoomed onto the main road out of the city. "Do they die with scared faces? Like Munch's *The Scream*, only with more hair."

Swift glanced at her briefly and Annie made *The Scream* face herself. He lifted the corners of his lips up at her, before pulling on a serious, work face. "That's what we're going to find out."

A silence washed over the car as they sped out of the city and headed to the small town just west of the ring road.

"I'm sorry you didn't get to have your party, Joe," Annie said, as Swift took the car off the main road and down a windy country lane. "We can rearrange it for another weekend."

Swift snorted. "No thanks. You were right, let's go to an escape room next time. Keep my house just for us, hey? And the rest of the MCU when they're behaving themselves."

"Deal," Annie said, laughing. "Where are we?"

Thornham Staithe was posh. Annie could tell as much as the buildings were all flint and brick and the verges were well maintained. They were driving through the town centre with shops named *Bluebell and Bracken*, *Pemberton & Co.*, *Frobisher & Figg* lining the cobblestone paved roads. Not a drop of litter blew in the wind, and the hanging baskets were enough to put Mrs Bucket to shame. Annie whistled through her teeth.

"Thornham Staithe," Swift said, indicating into the car park that was as neat as the rest of the town.

"Second homes for the London lot?" Annie asked, getting out the car and stretching her arms up to the blue sky. The town was empty, save for a couple of dog walkers who tipped their caps at the detectives.

"No," Swift said. "Apparently they've got a covenant that if you buy here, you live here."

"Nice," Annie replied. "I think I'm going to like the residents of Thornham Staithe a lot."

Eliza's studio was on the top floor of a converted barn, its brick and flint façade pristine despite the battering of wind and rain it must get being perched on the top of the only hill in Thornham Staithe. Annie puffed as they reached the door, but the view across the beautiful town was worth the slight ascent, which was a lot in Norfolk. A police car and a coroner's van were parked outside, their presence incongruous against the trendy café and bakery on the ground floor of the building. The whole area had been cordoned off, but there were no onlookers trying to rubberneck a glimpse at what had happened.

"Why didn't we park up here?" Annie asked, as Swift held the door open for her.

"I fancied some fresh air," Swift replied, heading into the building behind her. "Plus, CSI asked us to. They're treating the carpark as part of the crime scene too. Makes sense, I can't see anyone walking up that hill before they commit murder. They'd be huffing and puffing too much to sneak up on Eliza."

Annie straightened her shoulders and tried to hide how much she was huffing and puffing. It didn't work. And the metal stairs glared at her like a dare as she placed a foot on the first step and hoped her legs would make it.

They were greeted at the top by a couple of uniformed officers and a lot more blue tape. Ducking underneath, Annie and Swift pulled on shoe covers and made their way across the wooden floorboards. The studio was a stark contrast to the rest of the converted building. High ceilings and tall windows flooded the space with pale light, but that's where the modernisation stopped. The whole atmosphere was heavy, a freezing chill that crept through Annie's clothes and pinched at her chest. There was a small electric heater in the corner, no radiators, no double glazing, no plasterwork and paint, no damp proof coursing, as far as Annie could tell. It was like the builders had stopped on the floor below and left the attic space like it had been back when the first flint has been set in lime mortar. The smell of oil paint and turpentine was overwhelming, and the air had a faint metallic tang that made Annie's tongue feel weird.

Eliza Warren's body was slumped in front of an easel at the far end of the room, her head tilted at an unnatural angle. A trail of oils splattered the floor around her, leading to an overturned stool and a shattered palette. Her face was twisted in an expression that wasn't so much fear as paralysing terror. Annie knew immediately why Evans had suggested Eliza had been scared to death. Annie felt the residual fear emanating from the old woman even as her body lay there cold and stiff.

Swift approached the body. Annie watched as he scanned the area, head swinging back and forth to take in the 360 degree view around Eliza. He'd be looking at what she saw in her final moments. Annie hung back, her attention drawn to the room's details: the canvases leaning against the walls, the cluttered table covered in brushes and jars, the faint hum of the old space heater, though she didn't believe it was still on given the frigidness of the air.

But it was the painting on the easel that held her gaze. It looked like an unfinished portrait of someone. A woman with pale skin and dark hair, her face partially obscured by shadow. The details were striking—sharp cheekbones, a delicate jawline, eyes that seemed to pierce through the canvas. Annie felt a strange pull toward it, as if the painted figure was demanding her attention.

"Annie," Swift called, snapping her out of her thoughts. "Come look at this."

She joined him by Eliza's body, trying to shake off the unease that had settled in her chest. Up close, the scene was even more unsettling. Eliza's hand was outstretched, her bony fingers pointing. Was she reaching for something? Pushing something away? A crumpled piece of paper lay just beyond her fingertips.

Swift carefully picked it up with gloved hands and unfolded it. The paper was smeared with paint, the writing faint and shaky:

She's always watching me.

Annie shuddered involuntarily, shaking her head as Swift tried to pass the paper to her.

"I'm not touching that," she hissed. "Even with gloves on."

"What do you make of it?" he asked instead.

"It's creepy, that's for sure," Annie said. "Who's 'she'? And what was Eliza trying to say?"

"That's what we'll have to figure out," Swift said grimly. "Maybe *she* was who was frightening Eliza?"

"Maybe," Annie agreed, taking a step back and straightening up again. "This place is giving me the heebie-jeebies. Do you not feel it?"

Swift shook his head, still focussed on the body.

"According to the first officer on the scene, Eliza's assistant arrived to find her boss like this. He took her statement, and we can go and chat to her too, but he said a couple of things stood out from that first meeting. What was it?" He sat back on his haunches and blew out a stream of air from pursed lips. "The assistant said that Eliza had been different lately. I'm sure she said distracted and paranoid. She kept saying she felt like someone was watching her, but she wouldn't explain. And, apparently, she wouldn't let anyone near that painting, either."

He pointed to the weird looking half finished portrait that Annie was trying really hard to ignore. Reluctantly, her gaze flicked to the portrait again. The woman's eyes seemed to glint in the light, almost as if they were wet.

"Did she mention who the subject of the painting was?" Annie asked.

"Don't know." Swift grimaced as he looked at it. "We can ask when we go and see her. And apparently Eliza was finishing up a few pictures for a new exhibition she was putting on. We need to talk to the gallery owner where she was showing. Can you see if you can find out any details about the gallery and the times of the show?"

Annie nodded. "What about this studio? Does anyone else have access?"

"Just Eliza and her assistant as far as we're aware," Swift said. "And possibly the gallery owner, because she's been collecting pieces for the show. But the assistant said she never came here uninvited."

Annie walked over to the wall where Eliza had stacked her paintings. They were beautiful, clever, and meticulous. Portraits of people from all walks of life. Annie admired the skill of the dead woman.

"What about these?" she asked Swift. "Do we need to track down all the models? Maybe someone took offence to their portrait."

It seemed a little far-fetched, but Annie knew the art world wasn't always as glossy as the pictures made it out to be.

"We can ask her assistant," Swift agreed. "Though they could have just asked her to repaint it if they weren't keen, surely? Right, I've seen enough, shall we go and talk to the assistant? She's waiting for us in the cafe downstairs."

Annie nodded as she wandered over to the unfinished portrait, drawn to it despite herself. The woman's face was hauntingly beautiful, but there was something off about her expression. Her lips seemed to twist slightly, as if caught between a smile and a sneer.

"Annie," Swift called. "Don't touch anything."

"I wasn't going to," she said, stepping away, surprised to feel her arm had risen and her finger was edging towards the woman's face. "But don't you think there's something strange about this painting?"

Swift gave it a cursory glance. "It's unsettling, I'll give you that. Maybe it's because it's not finished."

Annie wasn't convinced. She glanced at the other canvases leaning against the walls, but none of them seemed to carry the same weight as the one on the easel.

"Something's not right here," she murmured.

Swift didn't reply. He was already heading towards the door to the stairs. Annie lingered, her gaze drifting back to the unfinished portrait. The light in the room flickered, casting strange shadows across the canvas. For a split second, she thought she saw the woman's lips move. A chill ran down her spine, but when she blinked, the painting was the same as before.

"Annie," Swift called, holding the door open for her.

She shook off the feeling and followed him to the stairwell, but the image of the portrait stayed with her, etched into her mind like a dark stain. And somewhere, deep in the recesses of the studio, a faint, mocking laughter echoed in the stillness.

THREE

THE CAFE WAS CLOSED, BUT CLARA CRESSWELL SAT nursing a cup of something hot, the steam rising up past her red, puffy face to the high ceiling above. She was in what looked like high end lounge wear, the type made from cashmere that hung well and felt like a cloud; her warm blonde hair was pulled back in a neatly done, messy bun. Annie pulled out an Eames knock off in a startling pink and sat down opposite the young assistant. Swift sat next to Annie. The sounds of police radios chattered through the building around them.

"Miss Cresswell," Annie started, "we're so sorry for your loss. Were you and Eliza close?"

Clara Cresswell sniffed and hid her face behind the large cup as she nodded. Closer, Annie could see that Clara was probably in her late twenties. She had a young face, but the steely look in her eyes was one that told of having lived a life.

"Clara, please," the woman croaked, sniffing some more. "And yes, we were. I've worked with Eliza for nearly five years. I know what she wants before she knows it herself."

"Can you tell us what happened this morning?" Swift asked, flipping his notebook to a new sheet and resting back in his chair. "How come you were working on a Sunday?"

"I'd messaged Eliza last night, there are so many things to organise in the run up to an exhibition that time off is scarce," Clara said, sipping her drink. "I didn't hear back so I thought I'd pop in on my way through to make sure Eliza had gotten it."

"Way through?" Swift prompted.

Clara nodded. "I live just a bit further up the hill and I was heading to Breadly anyway, they do the best cob loaves."

Breadly Thatch. Annie had seen the sign for the bakery next door to where they were sitting and thought it had sounded as cute as the names of the independent high street stores.

"What happened when you got here?" Swift asked.

Clara chewed the skin on her bottom lip until it was red raw. She twisted her hands around the handle of the mug, picking at her thumbnail absentmindedly.

"I saw there was a queue for the bakers so I thought I'd wait there first, Sundays are busy days and I didn't want to miss out on the cobs." Tears fell down Clara's cheeks. "I feel awful about that.

Knowing that I was waiting for bread when Eliza was up there…"

Her words fell away as her bottom lip wobbled. Annie reached out a hand and gently rested it on Clara's, motioning for her to put the cup down before it spilled everywhere.

"Even if you'd gone straight up to the studio, it would have been too late," Swift said, kindly. "There was nothing you could have done for Eliza. She was already gone."

Clara nodded thankfully at the DI.

"So, you got your bread, and then what happened?" he coaxed.

"I, um, well I popped it in the car and then came back in and went up the stairs to the studio. It was freezing up there, colder than normal. Eliza has this old heater that I'm surprised she's allowed to use in a building so old and with businesses underneath, but it's hers so she does what she likes." Clara's eyes widened. "Did what she liked."

"Eliza owned this whole building?" Annie asked, trying and failing not to let the surprise show in her voice.

Clara nodded again. "She only ever used the top floor, so when the developers asked if they could refurb the rest of the building, she didn't have an issue."

"How long ago was this?" Swift asked.

"Oh, ages, like years. Eliza was pleased that someone else would be managing the old stone masonry because it meant that she didn't have to worry about it falling down around her ears. But she was a little put out when they only did the ground floor."

"Understandably," Annie agreed. "So they left her without heating, is that why it was cold when you went up to see her this morning?"

Annie remembered how her breath had fogged in the studio as the little heater lay dormant. She couldn't imagine how a woman of Eliza's age was able to stay warm in those conditions.

"Weird thing was the heater was full blast. It should have been stifling up there. But when I went in and saw her on the floor like that, it was like her body was sapping the heat away." Clara wiped her face with her sleeve. "Sorry, that's weird, isn't it? I'm still trying to process what happened."

It wasn't weird though, Annie had felt the same. Except Annie had thought it was the painting leaching the heat away, not Eliza.

Outside the large windows of the cafe a gurney trundled across the shingle, pushed by the pathologist, Evans, his shock of pink hair stark against his white overalls.

"Excuse me a minute," Swift said, getting up and heading out to meet Evans.

Annie turned her attention back to the assistant. Her skin had paled, and she looked a little clammy.

"Do you have someone at home so you're not alone?" Annie asked. "You've had a shock."

Clara nodded sadly. "But I felt closer to Eliza than my own family, really. My mum and dad can be quite insular. What am I going to do?"

There was a void waiting for Clara now. A woman who seemingly put her whole life into her work. Annie just hoped she had friends locally who could rally around and help.

"You'll need to stay here for the time being," she said. "An officer will be along to take a formal statement, and the paramedics will want to check you over again. Is there anyone you know who would wish Eliza dead?"

"No." Clara's shout made Annie jump a little in her seat. "Sorry, no. Eliza had no enemies."

"And what about family?"

"No one that I knew of," Clara replied, settling back into her chair. "I did everything for her."

"Then she'll need you now too, even though she's passed away, if you're able?" Annie said, softly. "There will be a lot of questions to answer and things to organise once we've released the studio."

Clara nodded, not looking at Annie.

"Just before we go," Annie added. "Can you please tell me more about this exhibition Eliza was prepping for?"

"It was supposed to be her last, though Eliza wasn't sure about that." Clara said before giving Annie the address of the gallery and the name of the owner.

Annie thanked her and headed back out into the

April sunshine just as Swift was descending the stairs from the studio.

"I'm worried about Clara," Annie confessed, drinking in the warmth of the sun.

"I've asked Tink to come up and take her formal statement," Swift replied, agreeing. "She's had a tough morning, and I know Tink is a friendly face. And I've also asked Tink and Page if they'll give the studio another look over while we go and speak to the gallery owner. Did you get the details?"

Annie nodded and they headed back down the hill to Swift's car.

The gallery was everything Annie imagined an art gallery to be—sleek and modern, with its pristine white walls and gleaming wooden floors. Art pieces hung, carefully positioned and lit, their colours popping against the minimalist background. It smelt posh, like room fragrance that was definitely out of Annie's price bracket.

They had driven about ten minutes out of Thornham Staithe to another, smaller town with better link roads to the main city. The gallery was on the main thoroughfare. Sandwiched between a car shop and a haberdashery. Annie wasn't sure which town they were in, but the shops here were a slight downgrade from the ones they'd left behind. This was more *Budgens* than *Bluebell and Bracken*.

Though *Greyfriars Gallery* was a notch above the rest.

Vivienne Hart, the gallery's owner, was a striking woman in her mid-forties, with silver-streaked dark hair pulled into a chignon. Her tailored navy suit was immaculate, but her trembling hands betrayed the composure she was trying to project.

"I still can't believe it," she said, her voice tight. "Eliza was... brilliant. She was complicated, sure, but aren't all great artists? She deserved better than this."

Annie and Swift sat opposite her in Vivienne's small, tastefully decorated office. Swift had his notepad out again, his pen poised. Annie, however, couldn't stop glancing at the painting just visible through the office door; one of Eliza's earlier works. A pair of hands, twisted and skeletal, reaching for something just out of frame. Though *Grayfriers* wasn't exclusively full of Eliza's paintings, they certainly took pride of place over the other artists.

Swift cleared his throat. "Ms. Hart, can you tell us about Eliza's behaviour in the weeks leading up to her death?"

Vivienne hesitated, twisting a gold bracelet around her wrist. "She was unsettled. More so than usual. Eliza was always a bit eccentric, but recently, she'd become paranoid. She talked about feeling watched, as if someone—or something—was in the studio with her."

"Did she mention anyone by name?" Swift asked.

"No," Vivienne said quickly. Then, after a pause:

"But she was obsessed with this one painting. The portrait of the woman. She wouldn't stop working on it, even when she should've been finishing pieces for the exhibition. She said it had to be completed, that it was the key to everything. I kept trying to persuade her to finish up the exhibition pieces as people have already bought enough tickets to sell out for all three nights, but she wasn't listening to me."

"What did Eliza think the painting was the key to?" Annie asked, leaning forward.

Vivienne shook her head. "She wouldn't say. But there was something... unhinged about the way she talked about it. Like it wasn't just a painting to her, it was alive."

Annie and Swift exchanged a look, and Annie felt her skin pimple with goosebumps. If it was the unfinished portrait that Vivienne Hart was talking about, then she'd felt the same way.

"Can you tell us more about this painting?" Annie asked, not really wanting to hear the answer.

"It was a portrait. Eliza didn't really like to show her work while it was unfinished, but I did manage to sneak a look at it when I accidentally picked it up along with the other exhibition pieces. It gave me the creeps to be honest. I was glad to give it back." Vivienne wrapped her arms around herself. "I felt like it was moving. Though, that's insane, of course."

She laughed, perhaps realising just how insane it sounded out loud. But Annie didn't think this woman was crazy. Unless they all were. Artwork was supposed to engage feeling, but this portrait was doing a lot of heavy work when it came to evoking fear.

"Did anyone have a reason to hurt Eliza?" Swift asked, shifting the subject matter away from the picture.

Vivienne sighed, her hands folding in her lap. "Eliza wasn't an easy person to get along with. She had a falling out with her assistant last year, but they made up eventually. And there was the collector, Mr. Brannon. He was desperate to buy the portrait, even unfinished, but Eliza refused. She said it wasn't for sale, no matter the price. He didn't like that."

"What else can you tell us about Mr. Brannon?" Swift asked, his pen scribbling notes.

"Edward Brannon," Vivienne said. "A wealthy art collector. He has a reputation for being persistent, shall we say. If he wanted something, he usually got it. He'd been after Eliza's work for years, but she always kept him at arm's length. Though I have reason to believe he visited her studio only a few days ago."

Swift nodded, his pen tapping against the notepad. "We're going to need his contact details."

FOUR

"Why do you think Clara kept her argument with Eliza a secret?" Annie asked as they drove back to the station.

They were waiting on the art collector's contact details, so Swift had asked the team to assemble at the station for a debrief first. Annie had whispered MCU Assemble under her breath as Swift had been on the phone with Page, picturing herself as Black Widow. She thought Swift would make a good Captain America. Page would definitely be The Hulk, and Tink would be Wasp. She was so drawn into her daydream of MCU as Avengers that Swift had had to poke her arm gently to make sure she was still with him, and she'd replied telling him she wasn't quite ready to sacrifice herself for the greater good. To his credit, Swift hadn't batted an eye-lid.

"Maybe she thought it might make her look suspicious?" Swift replied, pulling into the station car park.

"Or maybe she just forgot. She'd had a shock; people's minds don't work well when they're struggling to just process the simple things needed to stay alive in those situations. This is your domain, Annie, you're a psychotherapist. What do you think happened?"

Annie hummed, getting out the car. "When she's had a little while for her adrenaline to stop pumping, I'd love to chat to her about that. It's not uncommon for assistants and their bosses to argue, but it could be something important."

"Sure. Good idea." Swift smiled his biggest smile and dropped his voice to a whisper. "Have I told you yet today that you're incredible?"

Annie felt like a schoolgirl as she grinned back at him. "Just the once, but feel free to say it again."

"You're incredible." Swift opened the door and stood back to let Annie go first. "And hot to boot."

Feeling her cheeks flush red, Annie stepped inside the station and kept her chin down as they walked past a group of uniformed officers who would absolutely have heard what Swift had just said.

"Don't forget Robins' threat," she said over her shoulder. "You're going to end up in Traffic if you're not careful. That was her last warning."

"Then she's going to need to come for me," Swift muttered. "Because I can't help it."

He gave her bum a squeeze and pushed through the doors to the open plan office. Annie took a moment to try and drop the grin from her face before she followed him. This wasn't really a time to go in all smiles and happiness. And from the look on Tink's face, the young DS agreed. She looked like thunder.

"What's up?" Annie asked, throwing her bag onto her desk. She dropped into her chair and swung it round to face Tink. "You okay?"

Tink and Page hadn't yet been out to the crime scene, though Annie knew they were heading there imminently. She wondered what the DS had been doing to make her so angry.

"Nope," Tink replied, shortly. "Not even a little bit."

"God, what's up?" Annie was concerned. Tink was normally a ray of sunshine, even on a bad day.

The DS cocked her head and narrowed her eyes at Annie. "I didn't get any chocolate, that's what's up."

Annie stifled a laugh as Page stood from his own chair and leaned over the screens to Annie.

"Trust me," he said, faux whispering. "You don't even want to know. She's been chewing a wasp ever since we got back here."

"Yes," Tink said. "Because we could have done the egg hunt first, then had delicious chocolatey goodness to keep us going while we were here searching the systems for Eliza and her associates. But I had to make do with Page's coffee and a stale biscuit from the staff room. It's Sunday. I was promised cake and sandwiches. No one is answering their phone, so it was a waste anyway. And do you know why they're not answering their phone, Swift? Because it's a Sunday."

Swift held his hands up in defence. Probably glad of the desk and computers between him and his DS.

"I can't help that people murder on a weekend. There's a vending machine in the lobby, why didn't you raid that?"

Annie could tell he was trying hard to not laugh too.

"A vending machine?" Tink stood up and leaned on the desk. "Have you seen what's in there? KitKats. Almost 100% wafer. I want easter eggs, the kind of chocolate that's the perfect thickness to be both melty and also substantial. There is a magic to them that is not to be found in a vending machine KitKat."

"Can't argue with that, Guv," Annie agreed.

Swift rolled his eyes. "Okay, look, you're right, Tink. Easter Eggs are gold tier chocolate. But we've also got the small matter of a dead woman who has the right to our full attention. So, sit your backside down and tell me what you've got."

Tink opened her mouth to retort, then must have thought better of it as she sat down with a thump and wiggled her mouse to awaken her computer.

"We've got Eliza's home address and found that she has no next of kin," Tink said, reading from her screen. "We've requested bank access and mobile phone records but they will take a while. No criminal record for either Eliza or her assistant, Clara. And there's no record of any calls to 999 from the studio or even the whole converted barn in recent history. Or any history, actually."

Swift nodded his thanks and turned to his other DS by his side. "Page?"

"We've delved into the art scene," Page started. "I wondered if it might be a bit cutthroat, you know, given how much some paintings can go for. But, on the surface anyway, there didn't seem to be any beef between Eliza and any other artists. She tended to keep herself to herself, from her socials. They were minimal, a couple of Facebook posts a year, no other platforms."

"She was in her eighties, wasn't she?" Annie asked, curiously.

"Late seventies, yep," Page confirmed. "But that's about the age of most Facebook users now, isn't it?"

Annie and Swift both gave the youngest member of their team a withering look.

"So there were no obvious competitors, or people with a vendetta," Page went on. "And I trawled the forums to no avail either."

"So we're probably not looking at another artist then?" Swift asked.

"Unlikely," Page replied. "It seems that, although Eliza could be prickly, she was kind and generous with upcoming artists and with her peers too."

Swift nodded. "Thanks guys. Anything else?"

"I tried to call your Brannon guy, we got his

details through pretty quickly once you sent the name," Page said. "There was no answer."

"Because it's Sunday and he's probably stuffing his face with easter eggs," Tink muttered under her breath.

Swift ignored her and looked to Annie.

"Anything to add?" he asked.

"Maybe," Annie nodded. "From talking to the assistant and looking at the studio I think we've got a paranoid artist, an obsessive collector, and an assistant who swears Eliza thought she was being watched and thought her paintings were coming alive as a warning. My gut feeling wants to say maybe dementia. Or some sort of neurological issues that made Eliza hyper aware and paranoid."

Swift glanced up at her, his expression questioning. "I can sense there's a but coming."

Annie smirked, thinking back to their arrival. She pulled her face straight. "You saw that painting. I think there's something off about it too. And I don't think I'm paranoid or suffering any neurological deficits."

"I dunno," Tink replied, grinning. "You're going out with Swift."

Swift raised an eyebrow. "Do you want to take a moment, DS Lock?"

Tink shook her head, actioning zipping up her lips. Swift nodded at Annie to continue.

"Like... I don't know. It's hard to explain," Annie admitted. "But the way Vivienne and the assistant talked about it too, it's made everyone feel weird, somehow. Like they were being watched."

"Watched?" Swift repeated. "It just looked like an unfinished painting to me."

"I'm just saying, it wouldn't hurt to consider the possibility that there's more to this than meets the eye."

Swift sighed, leaning back in his chair. "We're dealing with a murder investigation, not a ghost story. Let's stick to tangible leads."

But Annie wasn't convinced. "Okay, but can we at least put the image out there, see if anyone can identify the woman so we know who the painting is of?"

"Yeah, okay, good idea." Swift clapped his hands together, a sure sign he was wrapping up their meeting. "Tink, Page, can you put the portrait on social media and see if we get a hit? We'll go and visit Brannon first thing tomorrow, and we need to search Eliza's house too. In fact, Page, once you've gotten the portrait sorted, you and Tink head out to do a preliminary look at Eliza's house."

"Guv." Page started typing away.

"Annie, you and I have something really important to do." He got out of his chair and motioned for her to do the same.

Annie followed his lead, grabbing her bag and skipping to catch up with him as he marched towards the door. She had no idea where they were going, but it looked like he was on a mission.

"Swift?" she called, halfway across the office. "Slow down, would you?"

"Come on, Annie," Swift called back. "Those Easter Eggs aren't going to eat themselves."

He gave out a bark of a laugh and ran to the door as Tink jumped up from her chair and started after him.

"You're the worst boss, ever," she screamed as the door swung shut behind Annie. "I'm asking for a transfer."

Annie took a moment to catch her breath in the carpark as Swift unlocked his car and offered her a lift.

"I hope you're going to bring all those eggs in for Tink tomorrow?" she said, grinning. "I'm going to head home, now. Sunday needs me and I'm going to do some more research on our painter, see what I can find out before we speak to Brannon in the morning."

"See you then, O'Malley," Swift waved goodbye. "And if there's any eggs left, I'll be sure to share them out to the team."

He blew her a kiss and got in his car. Annie started the short walk from the station to her flat, relishing being out in the sunshine after still feeling the effects of the chill from the studio. Eliza's paintings had all been incredible. She was a painter who knew her way around a face. But Annie was sure there was something not quite right about the unfinished portrait, and she was sure it wasn't just her imagination.

As night fell, Annie sat in her pullout camp bed, her laptop fighting for space beside Sunday the cat on her knees. She'd spent hours researching Eliza Warren, poring over old articles and reviews, but the details were sparse. Her work was sold worldwide, but not much was known about the woman behind the portrait paintings.

She leaned back, rubbing her temples. That portrait was still nagging at her, a feeling she couldn't shake. She logged into her work emails and pulled up the photo of Eliza's unfinished portrait from the crime scene photos in her case files.

Heart pounding, she zoomed in on the painting, her eyes drawn to the woman's piercing gaze. The skin on her scalp tightened, sending a trickle of fear through her hair and down her neck. A streetlight outside her window flickered briefly, drawing her eyes away from the screen to the window and the streets outside. Sunday shifted, wobbling the laptop with his giant backside. He gave a little mew and jumped down to the floor, scuttling away and leaving a cold spot where his fluffy body had been. Annie turned back, bereft and a little frightened. The flat had grown dark around her, the streetlights the only source of light.

On her screen the woman in the painting seemed to be looking directly at her.

Annie swallowed hard, her chest tight with unease. Somewhere, in the quiet of the room, a faint sound echoed; a soft, lilting laugh. She spun around, but the room was empty. The laugh faded into silence, leaving only the flickering streetlight and the chilling weight of the woman's stare through the laptop screen.

FIVE

MONDAY

ANNIE WAS KEEN TO GET UP AND OUT OF THE FLAT the next morning which was unlike her. She'd slept fitfully, waking with every creak and groan from the old building and practically jumping out of bed with her laptop as a weapon when Sunday decided he wanted to sleep on her pillow. She was washed, dressed, and breakfasted by the time she walked to the station to meet Swift, but how awake she was was anyone's guess.

Luckily, Swift was driving the thirty minutes to Brannon's house. The sun was shining. And Annie spotted two takeaway Starbucks in the drink's holder of Swift's 4x4 as she leant against it in the carpark, waiting for her boss to appear. He bundled through the door just a couple of minutes later and greeted Annie with a smile and a kiss on the cheek.

"Sorry, I was just prepping Tink and Page; they're off to Eliza's house to see what they can find." Swift unlocked the car and they both climbed in. "I got you a flat white with caramel syrup, looking at you, maybe I should have made it a double shot. What's up?"

"Didn't sleep very well, that's all," Annie said, taking a swig. "That's sweet, sweet nectar though, thanks Joe. Right, tell me what we've got."

Swift watched Annie for as long as was safe given he was reversing out of his parking spot and heading out into the city.

"Sure you don't want to talk about why you didn't sleep very well?" he asked, gently. "Was it the fold out camp bed? There's a giant king size waiting for you at mine, you know?"

"I love my fold out bed," Annie protested, feeling her back twinge as she moved. "Though I think the springs are going. I might need to invest in some new ones."

"New springs?" Swift laughed.

"Yeah," Annie confirmed. "It won't be the first time they've been replaced. I've had that bed for as long as I've had my little flat. Neither of which I'm ready to give up just yet."

"No probs," Swift said, cheerfully. "But I won't stop asking."

"And I won't stop saying no." Annie looked at the DI and gave him a grin.

Maybe one day she would say yes, but not yet. She had toyed with the idea of using the flat as an office, which is what it was designed for. Maybe she could do a little consultancy work on the side, if the constabulary let her. She wouldn't have to keep her clothes in a filing cabinet or shower in a cubicle not even big enough for a mouse. Maybe one day.

They drove in comfortable silence, Annie switching the radio from BBC Two to One, and feeling the coffee running through her veins and keeping her alert. As they drove the sun rose higher in the sky burning away the dew from the field with a smoky haze. Popping her window down a notch, Annie felt the warming air on her skin and closed her eyes to enjoy the feeling. It was only as Swift turned off the engine and prodded her gently in the arm that she realised she'd fallen asleep. Thankfully, Swift had taken her coffee cup and put it back in the holder. Turning up to interview a suspect with a wet lap probably wasn't the best look.

Edward Brannon's estate was every bit as grandiose as Annie had expected from the Google search she'd done. A little further along from Thornham Staithe, it was found down a long, tree-lined drive that led to a sprawling mansion; its stone façade weathered to a tasteful patina. Annie rang the bell and the pair waited patiently for someone to come to the front door. Birds tweeted in the trees and a butterfly flittered by Annie's face. Spring was in full bloom and did wonders for Annie's wellbeing.

Brannon himself was as polished as his home. A tall man in his sixties with salt-and-pepper hair and the kind of confidence that came from years of wealth and power. He greeted them with a wary smile and, after Swift had introduced them, invited them inside where every wall seemed to be lined with priceless artwork, each piece lit by strategically placed gallery lights. They were led through to a sitting room, and Brannon gestured for them to take seats on leather armchairs that looked more expensive than Annie's entire existence.

"I understand you're investigating poor Eliza's death," he said smoothly. "Tragic, truly tragic. She was a genius."

"We understand you were interested in purchasing one of her works," Swift began, his tone neutral.

"Interested is putting it mildly," Brannon admitted, a faint smile tugging at his lips. "I wanted that portrait, more than any other piece she'd ever created. There was something transcendent about it. But she refused me. Repeatedly. Which was strange as I have a great collection of hers already. I imagine they'll be appreciating in value as we speak."

Nice. Annie bit her tongue but her face couldn't hide what she was thinking.

"I am sad, of course," Brannon added, his eyes on Annie. "But as an art collector I'm afraid I have a very narrow train of thought when an artist dies. I shall try to do better."

"Were you angry that Eliza refused to sell you the portrait?" Annie asked, watching his reaction carefully.

Brannon's smile didn't falter. "Frustrated,

perhaps. But angry? No. I respected her decision, even if I didn't agree with it. I heard she was becoming unwell," Brannon said, his voice dropping slightly. "Talking about strange things, claiming the portrait was cursed. I found it sad, really. Such a brilliant mind unravelling. It may have been for the best if she would have just sold me the damned thing; perhaps her mind may have quietened without the portrait in the studio."

"But it wasn't finished." Annie watched as Brannon pulled the sleeves of his jacket down over his wrists.

"No, no it wasn't," he agreed. "But it's incredible as it is, wouldn't you agree?"

Annie didn't agree, nor did she think it common that an art collector would buy an unfinished piece.

Swift cleared his throat, his pen moving briskly across his notebook. "Where were you the night of her death, Mr. Brannon?"

Annie knew he'd thrown that question in to catch Brannon off guard, watching carefully to see the man's reaction. But Brannon didn't flinch.

"At home," he replied without hesitation. "I had dinner with my wife and spent the rest of the evening in my study."

"We'll need to speak to your wife to confirm that," Swift said.

Brannon's smile tightened, but he inclined his head. "Of course. She's otherwise engaged at the moment, sleeping, but I shall pass on your details and

I shall call you when she's awake and free to talk to you."

Swift stood and handed the man a card. "Thank you for your time, Mr Brannon."

"I'll see you out," he replied, getting up and waiting politely for Annie to take her cue.

He led them back through the wide hallway to the front door in silence, his slippered feet shlepping on the wooden floors. When they got to the door, he stopped and turned back to the detectives, looming over them.

"Could you please be so kind as to put in a good word with the executors of Eliza's will. I really do wish to add that portrait to my collection." Brannon swung the door open, standing in the way of the exit.

Annie moved to leave but Brannon didn't shift from his position in the doorway. He raised his brows at her, questioningly.

"No," she said, shaking her head. "I won't. Now can you please let us leave?"

Swift was still laughing under his breath as they got back in the car to leave. He was scrolling on his phone, tapping out a message.

"He was a piece of work." Annie stabbed her seatbelt into the socket. "She's not even cold yet and all he can think about is the value of his collection and getting his hands on the unfinished one. I'd take the bloody awful thing home with me if it meant he didn't get it."

"I thought you liked her work?" Swift asked.

Annie remembered the whispers around the flat from the previous night and her body shivered. "I like her other pieces. That one, not so much. Where to now?"

Swift pocketed his phone and put the car in drive. "Page left a voicemail. There's something they need us to see at Eliza's."

By mid-morning, the MCU were gathered together in Eliza's home. The artist's house was as eclectic as the studio space had been—walls lined with mismatched bookshelves; every surface cluttered with curiosities. The air inside was cool, carrying the faint scent of old wood and oil paint. They congregated in the small study at the back of the cottage, which was not quite large enough for the four of them to stand with personal space between them.

"Talk to me, what do you have?" Swift said, shuffling closer to Annie. "Why are we here?"

"We found this," Tink said, turning to the side and indicating pen scrawl on the wall behind her.

Annie read around the bodies of her team, her heart quickening as she went.

They looked like diary entries. They started out normal enough—notes on commissions, ideas for new projects—but as the weeks progressed, the tone shifted.

March 3rd: I dreamt of her again. She

was standing in the studio, watching me. I couldn't move.

March 10th: The painting is almost done, but something's wrong. Her eyes... they're different now. I didn't paint them that way.

March 15th: She knows what I've done. I see it in her eyes. She won't let me forget.

"What the heck?" Annie whistled through her teeth; her voice unsteady.

"This could just be the ramblings of a paranoid mind," Swift said, though his voice lacked conviction.

"On a wall?" Annie agreed. "She says, 'she knows what I've done.' The woman in the portrait, right? Who is she?"

Swift nodded slowly. "That's the next thing we need to find out. I don't suppose you found anything to indicate who she is buried in the paperwork here, did you?"

Tink shook her head. "I spoke to Clara on the phone, arranged a time to go out and take her formal statement. I did ask her if she knew about the model of the portrait, but she said something weird like, what was it now, she thought it was someone from Eliza's past who was making her feel guilty."

"Guilty?" Swift probed.

"Yeah, that the painting was her way of making amends."

"Right, okay, we really do need to find out who this woman is." Swift ran a hand through his hair and puffed out his cheeks. "Anything else?"

"There's a lot to go through," Page added. "We've found bank statements that suggest our victim wasn't in any kind of financial trouble. Quite the opposite. She also has a rather large stash of cash under her mattress. Nothing to suggest Eliza had any enemies or…"

"There was one other thing, though," Tink interrupted. "Sorry Page, it just occurred to me. There's a space in Eliza's bedroom on the wall that looks as though a painting has been recently moved. The sunlight has bleached the paper on the wall, all except a square of paper that looks like new, just a bit cobwebby."

"Do you think Eliza moved it?" Annie asked.

"Don't know," Tink replied. "All we could tell was that it's not here, in the cottage, I mean."

"That's weird." Annie screwed up her face. "Do you think maybe there was another painting that she was paranoid about? Did Clara ever come here? Can we ask her what's missing?"

"Good idea," Tink agreed. "I'll ask her when I see her later. Actually, I'd best be off now if I'm going to get to the studio on time."

Annie started to edge her way out of the study, she wanted to look at Eliza's safe spaces, where she lived and how. It always told her a lot about the way a person's mind worked. She made her way through the low-ceilinged living room and into the smallest kitchen she'd ever seen, and that was including her own. There was no cooker, no washing machine, no dishwasher. It was a hob and a table and a small sink with a curtained cupboard underneath it.

She pulled out her phone, intending to take photos for the case, but as she did so an image appeared on her Home Screen. A photo of Eliza's studio taken from a strange angle, as if someone had been standing in the corner of the room on a chair.

Annie's stomach tightened as she stared at the screen. She clicked the photo message, and the caption read:

You're looking in the wrong places

Her blood ran cold. She opened her mouth to call Swift through. But when she looked back at her phone, the photo was gone.

SIX

ANNIE FLICKED THROUGH THE APPS ON HER PHONE, trying to find the photo, but it was gone. Vanished completely.

"What the heck?" she muttered, then shouted for Swift. "Swift, come and see this."

Swift was by her side in a matter of seconds and Annie held out her phone so he could see the empty MMS screen.

"Someone just sent me a picture of Eliza's studio," she told him. "Said we were looking in the wrong place."

Swift leaned in. "What? Let me see."

"That's the thing though," she uttered. "I clicked on it and it's not there anymore."

"It was here and now it's not here anymore?"

"Nope, yep." Annie locked and unlocked her phone again, but the image had well and truly vanished. "Maybe it was a new thing. Vanishing messages, like Snapchat, or whatever the kids are using these days." She frowned. "But why send me the picture in the first place?"

Swift frowned. "What was it a picture of, again?"

Annie glanced at him, pulse fluttering unevenly in her neck.

"Eliza's studio, taken from inside. But it wasn't just a picture. Someone had typed that we're looking in the wrong place. And the picture was mainly of the unfinished portrait from Eliza's studio, rather than the studio itself."

The painting they hadn't been able to identify. Someone had sent it to her. Someone who wanted her to see it. And now it was gone. A deliberate move. A warning? A clue? A taunt? Annie wasn't sure, but she felt as uneasy about the photo message as she did about the portrait itself.

Swift exhaled through his nose. "Right. Tink and Page are heading to meet Clara to take her statement. Forensics are coming here to bag up anything of interest and take pictures of Eliza's diary wall. We'll go back to the station and run down every possibility. Let's see if we can get the tech team to look at your phone and find out who sent that message."

Annie nodded, slipping her phone back into her pocket. "I want to go back to the studio."

"Me too," Swift said grimly. "But before we do, I want to know who's in that portrait. And I think our best bet is to look at the calls we've had since Tink put the image up on socials. Come on, we can get a Maccy D's on the way back to the city."

By the time they returned to the station, the open plan office was alive with activity. Officers filtered in and out, case files piled high, the incessant trill of ringing phones and notification beeps made the voices louder and the chaos more chaotic.

"Wow," Annie said, fighting her way to her desk. "I forget what Mondays are like, despite the fact it surprises me every week."

Swift was waylaid on his way through the office by someone asking too many questions, so Annie set to work emailing tech and asking the likelihood of being able to recover a disappearing MMS. There was a stack of messages to wade through from the call-out for identification of the portrait. Annie lifted the pages and started at the top of the first one, almost immediately putting a cross through the tip off that the woman was an alien species who was infiltrating Earth looking for a new food source. Some people had too much time on their hands. And Annie was definitely not one of them.

After what felt like an age, Annie dropped her pen onto the pages and looked up, surprised to see Swift hard at work opposite. She'd gone through the top three sheets of paper and the other seventeen seemed like too much to face before another cup of coffee.

Annie threw a balled up Post-It note at Swift to get his attention. It bounced off his forehead and he looked up, startled.

"Why do the general public think it's okay to call a hotline specially reserved for the mystery of a poor dead woman—murdered woman—to tell us that their dog is the spitting image of the portrait and can they buy it?" Annie dropped her head into her hands and raked her fingers through her hair. "I'm going to get a coffee, can I get you anything?"

"Some more Post-Its?" Swift replied, grimacing. "I thought it would be best if we went through the tip-offs ourselves, given that we've seen the portrait, but I'm starting to regret my actions. Listen to this 'It's not an unknown identity, it's Taylor Swift' or this 'I saw a woman just like that at the fish counter in Tesco's last week. Could be her?' and this one for the win 'I'll pop it in my local Facebook group, there's a woman there who found a cat that'd been missing for over two months, she's your best bet at finding out who this woman is'."

Annie laughed. "Maybe we should invite that woman to join the team."

Annie's desk phone rang, she was still chuckling away to herself as she picked it up and answered.

"O'Malley."

"Hey stranger." It was Rose, the receptionist and Annie's long-term bestie. "There's a guy in reception asking to speak to either you or Swift."

"What about?"

"About the painting," Rose replied. "Not sure what he meant, to be honest. I assumed you'd know. He was very specific about talking to you or Joe."

"Does he think it's Cheryl from Bingo?" Annie laughed. "If so, you can tell him that it's probably not and we don't really need to talk to him."

"What?" Rose sounded confused. "No. He's very insistent, I think you need to come and get him."

"Okay, I'm on my way." Annie hung up and conveyed the conversation to her boss.

"Bring him up to Interview One," he said. "I'll go make sure it's presentable."

Annie nodded and headed out of the open plan office to the reception area, walking straight to the desk to talk to Rose. There were a few people sitting on the plastic chairs waiting to be seen and Annie didn't want to collect the wrong one.

"Hey, love," Rose said, chirpy as ever. "How's my favourite psychotherapist-cum-police detective doing today?"

"Afternoon, Rose." Annie smiled. "Sorry again that we had to cancel yesterday, I was looking forward to catching up over a chocolate hunt and a cuppa. Crime doesn't follow a nine to five. Right, where's my guy?"

Rose waved her hands, dismissing Annie's apologies. "Don't mention it, catch up soon though, yeah. He's the smart one with the pocket watch."

Annie span around and looked at the row of people sitting waiting. She picked her man out almost instantly. He was in his seventies, his hair flecked with grey, dressed in a dark woollen suit that looked expensive but well-worn, the watch fob hanging from his breast pocket. He sat stiffly, his gaze scanning the room as though he was bracing for something.

Walking up to him, Annie held out her hand. "Annie O'Malley, sir," she said as he stood. He was taller than her, unusual in a man of that age. "How can I help?"

He took her hand in his and shook it. His skin was warm and soft, but his grip was firm.

"I wondered if I could talk with you about a picture my grandson showed me this morning?" He was well-spoken enough to carry a certain weight to his question.

"Of course," Anne agreed. "If you'd like to follow me, my colleague is waiting with a room. Lovely weather we're having, isn't it?"

The man didn't take Annie up on her offer of small talk, so they walked in silence through the corridors to the interview rooms. Glad that Swift had picked Interview Room One, given it was the only one with windows, Annie opened the door and motioned for the man to go on ahead. The sun was casting a square of light on the table in the middle of the room. Swift greeted the man with a handshake and an introduction, and they all took a seat.

The man's grey eyes were watery, but Annie wasn't sure if it was his age or emotions that were the cause. She sat with Swift as they waited for him to speak.

"My name is Dominic Grayson," he said. "I'm here about the picture. My grandson showed it to me this morning and I came straight away."

Annie straightened. "Do you know who it is?"

Dominic's lips pressed into a thin line. "A long time ago." He hesitated.

Annie and Swift exchanged a glance as Dominic reached into his suit jacket and pulled out a worn, creased photograph. He held it out, his fingers gripping the edges like it might slip away. Annie took it, smoothing it out on the table.

The air seemed to shift around them.

A young woman stared back at her from the photograph—hauntingly familiar. Annie's pulse kicked up a notch. Her brain was screaming at her to look away from the photograph, but she couldn't. A cold, dripping sensation flooded her head and painfully stabbed behind her eyes. She tried to blink it away but ended up blurring the woman in the photograph.

The features. The shape of her face. The intensity in her eyes. It was her. The woman from Eliza's unfinished portrait. Though she looked a good couple of decades younger.

Annie's mouth was dry and sticky as she spoke. "Who is she?"

Dominic's jaw tensed. His voice, when he spoke, was low.

"My sister." His eyes flickered between them.

"Your sister?" Swift repeated.

Dominic nodded.

"Do you and your sister know an Eliza Warren?" Swift asked.

"I know of her," he said, pointedly.

Annie got the feeling that there was no love lost between Dominic and Eliza.

"And what about your sister, what is her name?" Annie asked.

"Margot Grayson," he replied. "Margot and Eliza were friends."

He didn't elaborate, despite the space both Annie and Swift gave him.

"Used to be friends?" Annie prompted in the silence that was left, picking up on the past tense of Dominic's words. "Did they have a falling out? Do you think your sister might have wanted to do Eliza harm?"

She might have overstepped the mark with that question, but Annie could tell that Dominic wasn't going to offer up information that he didn't need to, which was weird given that he'd come to see them rather than the other way around.

"I don't know," he replied. "Does the painting belong to Eliza? Is that why you're asking me about her? Is Eliza the reason you were asking about the painting on social media platforms for anyone to see? Did you not think about how it would make people feel?"

For a split second, Annie thought Dominic meant that the painting made everyone feel as chilled and uneasy as it had her. That they shouldn't have put it out into the world because now everyone would be having the same nightmares she was. Then she remembered this woman was his sister and thought better of saying how creepy she was.

"Mr Grayson." Swift sat forward and steepled his fingers. "We really appreciate you coming in and identifying the woman in the portrait. It's very helpful for our investigation. Now, if you'll excuse us, we really do need to be getting back to work."

Dominic Grayson didn't make a move to leave. He looked vacant, staring out the window into the sunshine and the blue sky and the occasional bird that flew high enough to be able to see.

"I don't know if my sister and Eliza had a disagreement," he said, eventually, his eyes cool. "And I don't know if Margot wanted to do Eliza harm. And I'm surprised at you asking me those questions."

"I'm sorry, Mr Grayson," Annie conceded. "We're investigating the suspicious death of Eliza, and we needed to get to the bottom of the woman in the painting."

"In that case, I hope you do a better job of this investigation than you did twenty years ago." Dominic sat back in his chair, the wind fallen from his sails.

"I'm sorry, what do you mean?" Swift asked. "What happened twenty years ago?"

"Margot Grayson happened. My sister vanished. She has been missing for twenty years. So you can imagine the anger I felt at seeing her picture being used to highlight her as a *person of interest* in a murder enquiry. She was no person of interest twenty years ago when your lot made no effort to find her."

SEVEN

Dominic Grayson had left them with a mobile number, a promise to call him if they found anything, and an uneasy feeling in Annie's stomach. The kind that was a constant anxiety, yet she couldn't put her finger on why she was worried.

"We need to dig out the original case files from Margot Grayson's disappearance," Swift said, as they walked up the corridor towards the incident rooms. He picked the first empty one they came across and opened the door, ushering Annie inside. "I'll get Tink and Page back here, we need to go over what we've got so far and tell them the news."

Annie perched on the edge of a desk, absently flipping through her notes, as Swift called the others and then set about scrawling on the whiteboard.

Eliza Warren. With her crime scene photo and print out of the portrait, the whiteboard was starting to give off a haunted look. The questions around her, the start of a spider's web of who/what/why? Money? Artwork? Accident? Swift filled the whiteboard with names, dates, and hastily scrawled connections. Clara Cresswell, assistant. Edward Brannon, the wealthy art collector. Vivienne Hart, gallery owner, and now Dominic Grayson, Margot's estranged younger brother. Annie searched the board for connections and questions she may not yet have thought of.

It wasn't long before Page and Tink strolled in, Tink balancing a paper cup of coffee and a sandwich precariously in one hand. She was a whirlwind of energy in her oversized blazer and scuffed boots.

"What have we got, boss?" she asked, dropping into a chair beside Annie.

"Plenty of questions," Swift replied, his tone clipped. "Not enough answers. Though we do have the answer to perhaps the second most pertinent question. Who is the woman in the portrait?"

"And who is she?" Page asked, his tablet on the table in front of him as he took notes. "Anything to suggest why it was so important?"

"That's the million-pound question," Annie said, setting her notebook aside. "And the answer could be yes. Margot Grayson, missing person."

"Missing?" Page asked, wide-eyed. "Since when? Could she be our perp? Run off after the event?"

"Not unless she killed Eliza over twenty years ago, then no," Annie replied.

Tink whistled through her teeth. "What a tangled web we weave."

"Alright, Walter Scott," Swift said. "Anything of use to add from your meeting with Clara?"

He held out the pen to Tink, but she shook her head, her hands full of sandwich.

"You go ahead," she said. "So, Clara confirmed that she was at home all evening when Eliza was killed. We've checked her records, and her phone was switched off for hours. No calls. No texts. No internet usage at all. So, the phone didn't ping on any locations. And, for someone who was glued to their phone during pretty much the whole chat, that's a bit unusual, don't you think?"

Swift nodded.

"Did she give a reason why she was offline?" Annie asked.

She was asleep, apparently. Not checking her phone." Tink took a big bite and nodded to Page to continue.

"We asked her about the painting missing from Eliza's bedroom." Page took over. "She didn't know what we were talking about."

"Not that unusual for an assistant to stay clear of their client's bedroom though," Annie interjected when Tink raised a brow. "Do we know if Eliza's will has an inventory of paintings? We night be able to narrow it down if we can get hold of it."

"Great idea," Swift acknowledged, scribbling their findings onto the whiteboard. "And good work, guys. Anything else?"

Page and Tink exchanged a look that Annie couldn't decipher.

"What?" Swift wasn't taking any prisoners.

"Well, it's just that Clara reiterated how scared Eliza was of the painting. She also said that it wasn't meant to be seen, that it had to stay hidden. It's all a bit weird, isn't it?" Page told them. "It's just a painting. I had a quick peek at it after we spoke to Clara and I don't get all the panic about it."

"Yeah, me neither, Page," Swift agreed. "But there we go, no accounting for other people's strangeness. Okay, Tink, Page, you two need to get the files from the Margot Grayson missing persons case, see if we can find out why Eliza is scared of her own painting of the woman. And can you also get a copy of the will to see if there's a list of paintings from Eliza's personal collection?"

"Guv." Page and Tink answered in unison.

"Annie," Swift went on, "we're off to see Evans, the autopsy results are starting to come in. And we need to check out Brennan's wife's alibi too, see if uniform can do that. Any word back from tech yet?"

Annie shook her head. "Nothing yet, though they did email to say a lot of stuff is end-to-end encrypted now so it's impossible to trace."

"Awesome." Swift ran a hand through his hair and traced a very thin line of marker pen on his forehead which made Tink giggle into her coffee cup. "Any more messages?"

"No," Annie replied, motioning to her own head

to indicate what he'd done. "But I'll try and screenshot if anything else comes in."

"What's this?" Page asked, as the whole team watched Swift draw another line on his face as he scratched his chin. "Guv, you're turning yourself into a Picasso."

"What?" Swift looked down at his hand and spotted the open marker. "Oh, crap. I'll meet you at the car, Annie."

He was scrubbing at his face as he left the room. Annie filled the others in on her disappearing message as soon as they'd all stopped laughing, which took a good few minutes.

Swift's forehead looked like the colour of a bruise by the time he walked back out to his car. The black marker and the redness of his scrubbing made for a bit of a mess.

"Not a word," he said to Annie, getting in beside her. "I've tried my best but they're hardcore pens."

"I wasn't going to say anything," Annie lied, grinning. "Do we know anything about the autopsy already?"

"No," Swift said, reversing out of his spot and heading to the hospital. "Evans didn't say much, only that the preliminary results are in."

"I wonder what the cause of death was," Annie pondered as they drove into the low-lying sunshine.

"Eliza Warren died of a heart attack." Evans sat at his desk eating a Double Decker and trying to one handedly tie his pink hair back from his face.

Giving up, he put his chocolate down on a pile of forms and whipped his hair into a ponytail.

"A heart attack?" Annie was surprised, though once the news started sinking in, maybe she shouldn't have been.

The twisted fear on Eliza's face, the way her body had been holding itself, as though trying to protect her face from something treacherous.

"Yep," Evan confirmed. "But that's not to say foul play wasn't involved, but you'll have to work harder now to prove it."

"Are the tox results back?" Swift asked. "Any signs of alcohol or drugs in the blood? Could a poison have caused the heart to fail?"

"Not back yet," Evans said. "But you'll be the first to know when they are. And yes, there are about a million toxins that can cause heart failure. Including, and not limited to, this bloody Double Decker. I can feel my arteries hardening with each bite. Talking of chocolate, my kids are gutted they didn't get to come hunt some down in the Swift-O'Malley residence yesterday. Save us some."

"You'll have to fight Tink for them," Swift shrugged. "In fact, I'm actually quite glad we had to cancel because I think she would have taken out your kids for a Cadbury's Caramel Egg."

"Wouldn't we all?" Evans noted, wistfully. "Wouldn't we all?"

"Do we have anything else to go on?" Annie asked, trying to steer the conversation back to Eliza. Her head had started aching the moment she'd woken up, and it had gotten worse as the day had gone on. So much so that bright lights were flashing in her peripheral vision like a dodgy nightclub strobe.

"Traces under her nails," Evans said, finishing his Double Decker and throwing the wrapper through a mini basketball hoop into the bin. "We're awaiting the compound results back, but it could have been blood. Red, crusty, you know the drill."

Annie nodded. "Anything else? Any defence wounds or signs of assault?"

"Nothing that I can see." Evans wiped his face with his hands. "Bruising to her coccyx, but that was probably from the fall. And the fall definitely didn't kill her."

"Shock of the fall?" Annie asked.

"Possibly," Evans said. "But unlikely. I think, from how the bruising was patterned, that she was dead before she landed."

Swift whistled through his teeth. "Shock of something else."

A sharp, stabbing pain shot through Annie's head and she winced at the coldness of it.

"You okay there, Miss O'Malley?" Evans asked, leaning over his desk.

"Yeah, just a headache, that's all. Swift, would

you mind dropping me back home? I think I need to lie in a dark room for a bit."

Swift immediately got to his feet, putting the back of his hand on Annie's forehead so tenderly she felt tears spring to her eyes.

"Are you okay? Can I get you anything?" Swift asked, concern on his face.

"I'm fine," Annie tried to laugh it off. "Just a sore head. I think I need to sleep, that's all."

"I'll be in touch as soon as I know any more," Evans said, watching them both leave with a fatherly nod of his head. "Take care, Annie."

Annie O'Malley had always loved the quiet hum of the city at night. The distant murmur of traffic, the occasional wail of a siren, the rustling of the wind through the alley behind her flat; it all reminded her that she wasn't alone, even when she wanted to be.

Tonight, though, the quiet felt different. She'd dozed in the dark on her small camp bed, waving away offers from Swift to stay. There was so much to do on the case, she didn't want to keep him away. But now, having woken to the dimming light of the day ending, she was questioning her choice.

She sat curled on her bed, laptop balanced on her knees, scrolling through case notes with one hand while the other absentmindedly scratched Sunday behind the ears. The cat purred softly, a comforting presence in the dimly lit room.

A single lamp cast a pool of golden light over the cluttered coffee table with its half-drunk tea, a notebook filled with scribbles, and her phone, which had been silent all evening. Until now.

The sudden vibration against the wooden surface made Sunday's ears flick. Annie reached for the phone, frowning as she glanced at the screen. No Caller ID. Her thumb hovered over the answer button. Instinct told her to let it ring out. But listening to common sense had never been her strong suit. She pressed accept.

"Hello?"

For a moment, nothing. Just static, crackling softly in her ear. Then, a voice. Low, distorted, mechanical almost.

"You're wrong, Annie."

Her grip tightened on the phone. "Excuse me?"

"You're looking in the wrong places."

The distortion made it impossible to tell if it was a man or a woman. But the voice carried weight. Whoever it was , this didn't feel like a prank call.

Annie forced herself to stay calm. "And who exactly am I talking to?"

Silence. Then the voice crackled back through the phone.

"You don't want to end up like Eliza," it said, ominously.

A chill prickled across Annie's skin. She sat up straighter. "Are you threatening me?"

A soft exhale on the line, then the click of disconnection. The room felt colder. Annie lowered the phone slowly, her mind racing. She could count on one hand the number of times she'd actually been scared in this job. Nervous? Sure. On edge? Daily. But actual, stomach-clenching, skin-tingling fear? That was new.

Sunday yawned, completely unbothered by the shift in atmosphere, and stretched out across Annie's lap. Annie exhaled, forcing herself to think. Whoever called knew about Eliza's murder. And they hadn't called her out of kindness. They were warning her to stay away from something. Which meant she was getting close. Close to what, she had no idea, but that was exactly why she couldn't stop now.

EIGHT

If Swift was annoyed at having to come out at eleven o'clock at night, he certainly didn't show it. He was knocking at Annie's door within twenty minutes of her calling, fresh faced and happy to see her.

She relayed the conversation, pacing the short length of her flat while Sunday flicked his tail from the camp bed, watching her like a judge overseeing a trial.

"Did you manage to record the call?" Swift asked from the kitchenette where he was making Annie a cup of milky, sugary tea.

"No," Annie replied. "There was no time, they'd rung off before I'd even realised what they were saying. It feels personal, Joe. First the picture text, now this. Why is someone targeting me?"

She slumped down on one of her old consultation chairs by the window, the night sky full of stars and a fingernail of moon so bright it illuminated a square of light through the panes.

"Let's get tech on it first thing tomorrow. We'll try and trace where the call came from," Swift said, placing a steaming mug on the table and taking the chair opposite Annie, but not before giving her shoulder a gentle squeeze. "Did the voice sound familiar? Maybe they're targeting you because they have your number, it could be something as simple as that."

"Maybe," she admitted. "I didn't recognise their voice. It was distorted. Couldn't even tell if it was a man or a woman."

"Deliberately hiding, then." Swift cradled his own mug. "Why hide their identity? If they think we're looking in the wrong place, and they're happy to tell us about it—even if they're doing it in a really creepy way—they could be on our side? Why not just come to the station and give a statement? Why all the cloak and dagger?"

"Maybe they're afraid. Look at poor Eliza. We need to work out what they're afraid of."

"Or who. Eliza was certainly frightened of something and I'm still not sure about it being a painting that's coming alive," Swift agreed, he opened his mouth to say more when his phone beeped from his pocket.

"Bit late to be getting calls, isn't it?" Annie asked, curious and a little bit jealous, she hid her blush behind her mug.

Swift drew out his phone and sighed. "Not work calls, it isn't, sadly." He hit the screen and answered the call with his name and rank.

Annie watched as expressions passed over his face as he listened to the voice on the other end of the phone. Surprise. Amusement. Then disgust.

"We'll be right there," he said, wearily hanging up and looking at Annie. "There's been a break in at Eliza's studio. You okay to come with me?"

The second O'Malley and Swift pulled up outside the barn housing Eliza Warren's studio, they knew something was wrong. Even without the flashing blue lights and the crime scene tape, the place looked a mess. The front door was swinging slightly on its hinges, the lock cracked open like a ribcage split wide. A pit formed in Annie's stomach as she stepped out of the car, her boots crunching against the gravel. The cold air carried a faint, acrid scent—oil paint, chemicals, something metallic. She knew they were heading up the stairs to the attic space, and she knew what she was going to have to face. The thought of seeing Margot's piercing gaze made her throat hot with bile. They ducked under the tape and headed up to the studio and Annie tried to remind herself it was just a painting, and it couldn't hurt her, but her reminders didn't work as well as she hoped they would.

The damage upstairs was just as bad as down. Swift confirmed with the uniformed officer at the door that the scene had been photographed and re-secured before turning on his torch and shining it at the entrance to the studio. The door up here was the same as the door to the barn, smashed in from the outside with a force that had taken it almost clean off its hinges. Splinters of wood scattered about and footprints in paint made a muddled mess of the floor. Annie pulled on a pair of latex gloves and pushed the door wide enough for them both to enter the studio. The beam of Swift's torch swept across the destruction, illuminating chaos.

It had been wrecked.

Paint had been thrown across the walls in wild, violent streaks. Canvases were slashed, some in jagged tears, others shredded beyond recognition. The old wooden floor was covered in the wreckage—ripped paper, crushed brushes, the splintered remains of a once-standing easel. Shattered glass crunched beneath Annie's boots as she took a step inside.

"This isn't a burglary, is it?" Annie murmured, taking it all in. "Whoever was here wanted to make sure nothing was left. It's so violent, it's heartbreaking, Swift. All of Eliza's works, ruined. Her legacy is gone. The pieces that hadn't been sold or hung in the gallery are broken. Why would someone do this? Who hated Eliza so much that they needed to vent it in such an angry way?"

Swift's expression was unreadable as he moved

through the room. He crouched near what had once been Eliza's workspace, brushing a gloved hand over a torn fragment of canvas. The destruction was absolute. Paintings lay in splintered frames, their surfaces slashed beyond recognition, the scent of turpentine and oil paint thick in the air. Annie felt her headache return with a vengeance almost as soon as she smelt it.

"This wasn't just a random act of vandalism," he muttered, agreeing with Annie's sentiment. "This was deliberate. It's almost like they've been methodical in their eradication of everything Eliza had made."

Annie moved past him, her boots crunching over broken glass and twisted metal. She crouched near the remnants of a shattered easel, carefully peeling back a loose section of torn canvas. Even through the ruin, she saw Eliza's meticulous brushwork, her even strokes and attention to detail. She felt the aggression of the vandalism and the unfairness for those who loved Eliza and who would now have this mess of paintings as their mementos.

She turned over another canvas, this one wiped out with a layer of thick red paint. It was like a blood stain across the face of a Dachshund. Surely no one could take issue with a teeny dog who had a face like an angel. A shiver passed through Annie like an earthquake, though the studio felt warmer than it had the last time she'd been here. Tiredness threatened to engulf her, and she stood and took a gulp of air to try and level her head. Outside the windows the lights of the police cars flashed a disco ball of blues. She could see nothing further than their warnings. No night sky, no roads with passing cars, no lights on in houses where people were sitting in bed reading or scrolling their social. It was like the barn existed in a bubble of blues and twos but that didn't make Annie feel any less disturbed about what was happening.

"I can't see a single painting that hasn't been destroyed," Swift called over his shoulder as he leant over a pile of portraits that had been doused in turps. "These ones look like Picassos now, the faces are all melting away. Anything where you are?"

"Nothing salvageable." Annie's head thumped in her skull. "Not that I've found so far, anyway. There are a lot of paintings here."

Swift nodded and went back to his search. Annie wasn't sure if he was looking for undamaged paintings or something else, and she was about to put that question to him when a thought hit her like a punch to the stomach.

Her breath hitched. "Joe."

Swift stopped what he was doing and looked back at Annie.

"Everything okay? You look like you've seen a ghost."

Annie swallowed, her pulse skipping. "The portrait. It's gone."

He stilled. "Margot Grayson?"

She nodded, standing and turning in a slow circle, taking in the wreckage. Yes, all of the paintings had been shredded or smashed or defaced, their frames reduced to twisted wood. But the unfinished portrait of Margot? Nowhere in sight.

Annie pulled her shoulders back, scanning the room with new eyes. She grabbed at the frames they hadn't already inspected but there was no sign of the portrait. Was that why it felt warmer? Why Annie hadn't felt the sharp gaze of the woman like before? They scrambled through the wreckage, carefully looking for scraps or remnants of Margot, but there was nothing. Only the easel the portrait had rested on, chopped to pieces on the floor.

They met in the middle of the room; Swift's face was dusty with fragments of torn paper and sweat.

"So this wasn't just a destruction of everything Eliza had painted," he said, wiping his brow with the back of his hand.

Annie shook her head exhaling sharply. "No. Are we thinking that whoever did this also took the unfinished portrait?"

"And then ransacked the place in the hopes we didn't notice?" Swift asked.

"Quite likely," Annie agreed. "Christ, that's awful. Who would want the portrait so much they'd do something like this?"

"We've got a whole list of people who knew about the portrait," Swift said. "Some of them loved it, most of them hated it."

"Do you think any of them feel strongly enough to do this for it? Kill for it?"

"Maybe. Let's get out of here. You're coming back to mine, and I'm not taking no for an answer this time"

"I wouldn't be giving no as an answer this time, thanks Joe."

Swift gave her a soft smile and nudged the door open with his elbow.

"I'll send in the SOCOs to do a thorough sweep for prints, but I doubt they'll find anything. It's all so messy."

"Maybe they'll have left a print in the paint?" Annie said, hopefully.

"Footprints, definitely," Swift replied. "We've got the pictures of those so we can start to look at matches. And we can hope that some of the oils were still wet on the canvas, that stuff can take days to dry. You never know, we might get lucky."

But as Annie traipsed down the stairs behind Swift, she felt anything but.

The night was cold when they left the barn. Annie pulled her coat tighter around herself as she walked toward Swift's car, her breath misting in the air. The silence out in the countryside was thick, she missed the hum of the city and the white noise of office chatter. No one was out here. The police car was empty, the officer still manning the studio door while he waited for the SOCOs. The forensic teams from earlier had long since left. It was just Annie and Swift and the ghosts of the crimes that had been committed.

And yet…

She had that feeling again. A weight of being watched. She stopped, turning slightly, scanning the barn and the fields beyond it. And there—just visible in the glow of the moon—a figure stood, barely detectable in the shadows.

They didn't move. Didn't run. Just watched. A prickle ran down her spine and she made to shout to Swift, but she blinked and then they were gone. The unease remained though, curling deep in her gut. Either someone was keeping a close eye on everything she was doing, or she was going insane.

NINE

TUESDAY

THE MCU DESKS IN THE OPEN PLAN OFFICE WERE caught in that strange, heavy quiet that came with working too many hours under bad fluorescent lighting. The scent of stale coffee lingered, and their workspaces were a mess of open case files, half-eaten biscuits, and scrawled notebooks. Annie had barely sat down before Swift turned to Tink and Page.

"I want any DNA from Eliza's studio fast-tracked. Can you get on to Evans and see what he can do? And check on the tox results while you're there."

Tink groaned, stretching like a cat. "Yes, Guv."

"I want every trace of forensic evidence from that studio cross-checked against unsolved cases. Open cases. Any cases we have going. Every painting fragment, every tool, everything that might give us a lead."

Page was already typing. "I'll put the request in now. Might take a while to get results, though."

"Just make sure it's priority," Swift said.

"Consider it done."

Annie leaned forward, rubbing her temples. The stolen painting changed everything. It had to be a clue to the motive behind Eliza's death. Someone wanted that painting so badly they'd go to the extent of trashing priceless works of art to get it. So it was likely that the painting held value that wasn't simply monetary to the person who had stolen it.

"So, I'm just thinking out loud here," Annie said. "But do we think that Margot's painting was stolen because someone was desperate to have it in their possession? Or because someone wanted to destroy it? Brannon or Vivienne could be the former, and there's a whole heap of people who could be the latter."

Tink clicked her pen rapidly, eyes flicking between her screen and the rest of the team. "Whoever took it, they knew exactly what they were doing. They didn't grab random artwork, didn't even bother with the ones that could have been worth something. They went straight for Margot."

"Yeah, good point." Swift pushed his chair back from his desk. "There was probably thousands of pounds worth of artwork destroyed last night."

Annie exhaled. "They didn't just want the portrait. They needed it."

Swift frowned. "Which means they knew about it before we did. Before we even made the connection between the painting and Margot."

Page glanced up. "What's our theory here? Someone kills Eliza, then comes back to take the painting. Maybe they were worried about DNA being on it, or something like that? Perhaps they bled on it, or held it, anything that would have left a trace."

Tink turned back to her screen, muttering, "Well, that's horrifying. Let's find out who it was, shall we?"

Page let out a long sigh, tapping aggressively at his keyboard. "No pressure."

"Any word on Eliza's mobile or bank records?" Swift asked.

"Yeah, report came back a few hours ago. There's nothing out of the ordinary," Tink replied. "Looks like Eliza uses her phone about as much as Page's grandma, which means it's stashed in a drawer and switched off. A couple of calls to Clara a few weeks ago, but that's about it."

"Great! And bank records?"

"Hefty balance," Page replied. "Very hefty balance. Large deposits of money from a number of galleries, including Vivienne's, were regularly made to Eliza's business account. Having said that, there are a few anomalies in her personal account. A couple of recent transfers to a source we're tracing, quite big sums. A couple of thousand each. Will let you know when we know more."

"Annie," Swift turned to her as he spoke. "Anything from Tech about the messages or the call last night?"

"I rang them when I got in," she said. "They're trying to trace the call."

"And the vanishing picture"

Annie screwed up her nose. "Nothing.

"Encryption?" Page asked over the screens.

"No," Annie shook her head. "Literally nothing. They can't find any record of me having received a message at that time. Even a vanishing one."

"Is that normal?" Swift asked.

"No," Tink replied. "There's normally a footprint at least. Even if they can't see what it's of. To have nothing at all is very strange."

"Which means we're looking at someone who has advanced skills in tech then," Swift said, resolutely, as Tink gave Annie a funny look.

Annie looked down at her bitten fingernails. She had already started to question the picture message she'd seen. Or hadn't seen. Maybe she was just tired. Maybe she was stressed. Maybe…

"Annie," Swift caught her attention. "No one is questioning you."

It was like he could read her mind. She hoped that his skills stretched to work readings only and not to some of the regular thoughts she had about him in general. Feeling heat rise in her cheeks she muttered a thank you and started to get up from her seat, needing a moment to compose herself and a coffee. But before she'd gotten as far as pushing her chair back a sharp knock on glass and a pointed cough made them all turn.

DCI Robins stood in the doorway of her office, her face stony. Annie had spent enough time around her to recognise when something was seriously wrong.

"Swift. O'Malley. In my office. Now."

Swift was already standing, and Annie followed as he walked towards the DCI's office, the team silent as they went. Not even Tink muttered a teasing *ooh, someone's in trouble* under her breath.

They barely had time to sit before Robins got straight to it. "Vivienne Hart was found dead in her gallery an hour ago."

"What?" A chill ran down Annie's spine.

"How?" Swift asked, voice clipped.

"Throat slit," Robins said. "And it wasn't subtle."

The air in the office seemed to thin. Annie opened her mouth to suck in great gulps.

"What is going on?" Robins continued. "We've had a break in to a building we should have still been watching. And now someone else involved in this case is dead. Keep your head in the game here guys. You don't need me to tell you that if word gets out you're letting things slip then one of you will have to go."

"We've been nothing but professional, Robins," Annie said, feeling like crying. "Someone is targeting us, well me. It's the case. It's got people's hackles up."

Robins stared at them, thoughtfully, for a few

moments. Long enough to make Annie feel naked and start squirming in her chair.

"Okay." She gave them a brisk nod, seemingly convinced for now. But the DCI still looked like she could use a shot of whisky, and it was only ten a.m.

Annie exhaled slowly. "I'm guessing the fact that Vivienne is dead is not the worst part of this conversation."

Robins shook her head. "No. The worst part is how they left her."

She slid a crime scene photo across the desk. Annie's stomach twisted the moment she saw it. Vivienne Hart was posed in front of one of Eliza Warren's paintings, her head tilted at an unnatural angle, her lifeless eyes staring at something only she could see. A brush had been placed delicately in one hand, and a smear of red paint—or maybe it was blood this time—streaked across the eyes and mouth of the canvas behind her.

"Oh my god," she murmured. "That's awful. Poor Vivienne."

Swift's jaw tightened. "This is a warning, isn't it? The way the eyes and mouth have been crossed out, what are they saying? Don't look. Don't speak. Who are they warning?"

Annie didn't want to think too hard about that, because right now, it looks like it was meant for them.

By the time they reached the gallery, the sophistication of the space had vanished, swallowed up by the grim reality of the crime scene. Gone were the delicate arrangements, the carefully curated lighting, the quiet reverence that had once defined this place. Now, it belonged to forensics.

Cameras flashed, illuminating streaks of blood against the polished floors. White-suited forensic officers moved methodically through the room, their hushed conversations blending with the occasional shutter click of a camera. The scent of posh candles and polished wood still clung to the air, but it was losing the battle against the coppery tang of fresh blood. It curdled at the back of Annie's throat, its sharpness a grim counterpoint to the artificial sweetness of whatever overpriced fragrance had been burning the previous evening.

She and Swift nodded their greetings to the uniformed officers stationed at the scene before stepping further into the grim luxury of the gallery and heading straight to their victim.

Vivienne Hart. Annie took a slow step closer.

Vivienne sat unnervingly still, her body arranged with deliberate care. Her back rested against the wall, arms draped elegantly at her sides, head tilted ever so slightly—she looked as though she were merely contemplating a work of art rather than being part of one.

It would have been easy to miss the brutality of it. Except for her throat, marred by a clean, deep cut and a waterfall of dried blood. The cut was sharp, there were no jagged hesitation wounds. No messy second attempts. Whoever had done this had been precise in their actions. A killer who knew exactly what they were doing. Or worse, one who had taken their time.

Annie's gaze flickered upward to the painting that had been vandalised, probably with blood from the victim below it. It loomed overhead. The colours of the painting, warm and rich under normal circumstances, had turned sickly and warped beneath the harsh forensic lighting. The subject was an older woman, captured in strokes of gold and ochre, the layers of oil were crisp and clean, the face a signature Eliza Warren portrait. But her eyes and mouth had been crossed through with blood strokes from a wide paintbrush still grasped in Vivienne's hands. At any other time, it may have made a statement, a modern-day painting. One that wouldn't have looked out of place in the Tate. But, given the circumstances and given that the blood was 100% real now Annie had seen it up close, it was hard to look at with Vivienne's body arranged beneath it.

"This feels overly gruesome," Annie murmured, the words barely escaping past her lips. "Are we looking at the same killer? Someone who had a vendetta against Eliza and Vivienne? Why present her like this?"

"Like I said back at the station, eyes and mouth crossed out seems pretty stark." Swift mulled over the words like he was posing the question to himself.

"Maybe she had seen something she shouldn't have? Was going to talk? I don't know. Maybe the killer is an artist themselves and felt the need to make this exhibition. I'm at a loss. But all I can say is that this feels more like a warning now I'm standing in front of it."

Annie agreed with that sentiment. "We need to stop whoever is doing this before someone else is turned into part of a macabre exhibition."

TEN

As Annie walked around the gallery, the blue lights flashing through the large front windows, she felt like she was in one of those interactive shows. The Van Gogh *Starry Night* or *Nature's Confetti* at the Outernet. Only this one was a horror show.

Eliza Warren's other paintings gave an eerie backdrop of hateful eyes and Annie kept her gaze on the floor as she headed to the offices at the back of the gallery. Shutting the door behind her and Swift, she was glad to be out of the strobing effect that often made her feel dizzy.

"Wow," Swift said, whistling through his teeth. "Not what I was expecting, I have to say. Makes you look tidy."

Annie scoffed. Vivienne's office was the polar opposite of her gallery. Though it was large, with a big enough window to not need to turn the light on, it was as though a Tasmanian devil had waltzed around the room and left a hurricane in its wake. Papers were scattered over every surface. Cups left out. Her desk was underneath a pile of folders and wires and pens. At least, Annie assumed there was a desk in there somewhere. It might have just been stacks of more clutter for all she could see.

Swift cleared a space and sat down on the chair, finding the mouse under a pack of digestives. He wiggled it and the screen came to life showing a collage wallpaper of pictures of Vivienne and what must have been her Cocker Spaniel.

"Someone needs to go check on the dog," Annie said, frowning. "Poor thing might not have anyone to look after it now."

"Don't get any ideas," Swift said, his concentration stuck to the screen and the log in page they were faced with.

"Sunday wouldn't have it," Annie agreed. "If I took any other rescue animals home, he'd eat them for breakfast. Swift, do you think that the killer made this mess in here, a bit like they did in Eliza's studio?"

"No," Swift said, and he sounded pretty certain. "This isn't the kind of mess we'd find from a ransack. Plus, they could have done the same to the rest of the gallery and not just this room. It looks like long term messiness and although it looks like she's working in a hovel, I can kind of see a method in her madness."

"Whatever you say," Annie said, arching a brow.

"No, look, sales receipts are by my left elbow, what looks like tax info up there by the can of Coke."

Swift tried typing as he spoke. "What do you think her password is?"

Annie sighed. "Any chance she used *artlover123?*"

Swift gave her a look.

"Fine," Annie muttered, rubbing her temple. "We need IT."

But before Swift could call for IT backup, Page appeared in the doorway.

"Won't need them," he said, already heading toward the desk. "I'm pretty sure we can get in with one of the passwords written right here in this little booksie."

He waved around a black leather notepad, smiling like the cat who got the cream. Tink followed, tossing a file onto the already overflowing desk. A few papers swayed with the movement, threatening to start an avalanche of documents, but Swift slammed his hand down to stop them.

"What is that?" he asked Page, furrowing his brow at Tink.

"It was at the till point," Page replied, hustling Swift for the computer chair. "Forensics passed it to me as I walked in, thought you might need it."

Swift shuffled out of Page's way and left him trying to access Vivienne's files while he rounded on Tink.

"And what's in that file?" he asked.

Annie picked it up from the desk and started to leaf through it. It was a large wad of bank statements.

"Came through just after you guys left the office," Tink said. "Check this out. It's the gallery's financial records. Turns out Vivienne wasn't just selling art—she was getting paid off. A couple of large transactions into the company, with no art attached that we can see. And some more regular payments, smaller ones but still not insignificant."

Swift's jaw tightened. "From who?"

Tink smirked. "Your favourite art-loving, rich bastard."

Annie exhaled. "Brannon?"

Tink nodded. "He's been sending regular sums of money to Vivienne for a few months now, but here's the interesting part—one of the largest transfers happened two days before Eliza was murdered."

Annie glanced at Swift. "Paying to keep something quiet?"

"Or paying to make sure something disappeared," Swift murmured.

"Or paying to ensure he ends up with the unfinished portrait?" Tink added.

Across the room, Page made a satisfied noise, and they turned to see him leaning back in his chair with a triumphant look on his face.

"I'm in," he said. "Now let's see what Vivienne was hiding. Emails first?"

They crowded round as best they could with not much clear floor space. Page worked quickly, navigating Vivienne's inbox with the sharp efficiency of someone who had used Gmail before and understood the weird way emails were ordered. Within minutes, the DS had pulled up a string of messages, some buried in older folders, some deleted.

Swift leaned over his shoulder. "Sort by sender. Look for Eliza Warren."

Page did, and within moments, the screen filled with back and forth contact between the two dead women.

Annie read the most recent one first.

From: Eliza Warren
To: Vivienne Hart
Subject: URGENT

Vivienne, I'm begging you. I don't care about the money. Just destroy the painting before someone finds it. I shouldn't have painted it at all. It was never meant to be seen. Please—do this for me.

It was sent two days before Eliza was found dead. A chill ran through Annie's spine.

"Is she talking about Margot's portrait?" she wondered. "Did Vivienne have it at one point? Maybe for the exhibition. That doesn't make sense, though, it wasn't finished."

Page scrolled further back, scanning another thread.

From: Vivienne Hart
To: Eliza Warren

Subject: You don't get to rewrite history

Eliza, you don't get to pretend this never happened. The painting stays.

Swift leaned in to the screen. "Pretend what?"

Page scrolled faster. "There's more."

From: Eliza Warren
To: Vivienne Hart
Subject: RE: You don't get to rewrite history

I know. But if that painting is found, everything comes out. Do you understand what that means?

Swift muttered something under his breath. "What was she hiding?"

Annie barely heard him. Her eyes were locked on one last email, half-buried in the archives. It was older, from months ago, but something about it made her pulse pound.

From: Vivienne Hart
To: Eliza Warren
Subject: Recent Exhibition Portrait

Why did you paint this?

Silence settled over the messy office. Only the faint sounds of the forensic team could be heard through the closed door. Annie stood back slowly, heart hammering.

"So was Vivienne blackmailing Eliza?" she said. "Possibly over the unfinished painting of Margot."

Swift ran a hand down his face. "And then they both ended up dead."

Page's fingers hovered over the mouse. "I've just thought of something."

"Care to share it with the rest of us?" Swift asked.

Page span around in the chair to face them all, a deep line between his brows.

"The painting is of Margot, the missing woman, right? The one that's been stolen," he started.

"Yes," Swift urged.

"How old was Margot when she went missing?"

"Twenty years ago," Annie replied. "I think her brother said she was in her thirties."

The room fell silent, and Annie had a sinking feeling of realisation as she knew what Page was about to say.

"Then why is the Margot from the painting much older?" the DS finished. "Like, old enough to look like what she'd look like now, if she hadn't gone missing?"

Eliza hadn't been just painting Margot as she remembered her. She'd been painting Margot as she saw her now.

Swift's phone sprang to life and he turned away to answer it. "Evans, what can we do you for? Tell me it's good news. Hold on, I'm with the rest of the team, you can tell us all at once."

He held his phone out to the room and switched to speaker so they could all hear.

"Hi guys. Depends on your definition of good news," Evans replied. "The DNA results just came in for the traces found under Eliza's fingernails."

Annie and Swift exchanged a glance. Evans loved a dramatic pause.

"And?" Swift prompted.

"Oil paint, soil, and human DNA. Not Eliza's," The pathologist sucked in a breath.

"Do we have a match with anyone else?" Annie asked, impatiently.

"Yes," Evans went on. "Yes we do. You might want to sit down for this."

Swift came back over to the deck and placed his phone on top of one of the precarious piles of paperwork. "Evans, I love you, man, but can you please just get to the point?"

The pathologist laughed down the phone. "Sure thing, boss, the DNA was a match to one Margot Grayson."

The floor under Annie's feet seemed to tilt. She caught the arm of Page's chair to balance herself.

"That's not possible," she said numbly. "Margot disappeared twenty years ago."

"The results do not lie," Evans replied. "And Margot had one brother and no other siblings, so it's not a long-lost twin's DNA we're looking at here."

Tink let out a slow breath. "Then someone's got a lot of explaining to do."

Annie's stomach twisted. Margot was missing, presumed to be dead. So why had her DNA been found at a recent crime scene? Swift signed off the call, thanking Evans, and turned to his team.

"This changes everything." He ran a hand through his hair. "So as well as quizzing Brannon on the payments he was making, we need to talk to Dominic Grayson again. And Clara. Someone must know something about the whereabouts of our missing person, and the missing painting. We find that. We find our killer."

"But I think they're going to stop at nothing to avoid that happening." Annie screwed up her nose, remembering the vanishing message, the distorted voice, and the figure watching her at the studio. "Especially now. I wouldn't be surprised if we find it on fire in a bin."

"I'm more worried we're going to find another person on fire in a bin," Page added. "Watch your backs guys."

Swift and Tink laughed at Page's insinuation, but Annie couldn't help but feel it would be her they'd need to extinguish.

ELEVEN

As the forensic team worked on the removal of Vivienne Hart's body, the MCU team stepped outside Greyfriars Gallery and into the bright sunshine to give the medical staff some space. Cars whizzed past on the road and the sound of engines revving filtered out of the showroom next door.

"Did you guys pull Grayson's MisPer file?" Swift shouted over the traffic noise.

Tink nodded, she started to tell them about what she'd read when Swift held up a hand to stop her.

"Let's move somewhere quieter," he shouted. "I can't hear you over the noise and I want to make sure I'm not going deaf in my old age."

They followed Page as he walked along the narrow pavement to a small patch of green space with a couple of benches and an old duck pond. There were no ducks, probably because there was no water. Annie tucked her coat under her bum so the wet wood didn't stain her trousers as she sat down. Swift sat next to her with Tink and Page on the bench to their right angle.

"What have we got?" Swift said, audible now they were tucked away from the road behind a scraggly looking hedge.

Tink took out her phone and scrolled to her notes app to give them all the lowdown.

"Margot Grayson: 34. Last seen on October 12, twenty years ago. Last known location was leaving an event in London. They give her height and weight and distinguishing features, or lack of them by the looks of it. Current status: Presumed dead, but no body was ever found."

"Yet her DNA has just turned up in our crime scene." Annie sucked at her teeth. "How?"

Tink shrugged. "Witness statements are thin. No CCTV, no sign of a struggle, nothing to suggest an abduction. Just... she was there, and then she wasn't."

"They pulled surveillance from traffic cams, nearby businesses, even bus timetables, but nothing showed her leaving the area," Page added. "It's like she just vanished into thin air. I've just emailed over a picture to you all, it's one I took of the case file photos that I thought you'd like to see."

Annie took out her phone and looked at the email. A grainy black-and-white image with a staple through the top of it captured a smiling Margot, caught mid-conversation, a glass of wine in one hand. Nothing about the picture screamed tragedy to Annie. Margot didn't look afraid; she was just a person enjoying a glass of wine at a function with a lot of other attractive people. She didn't look like someone who wanted to vanish off the face of the planet.

Tink tapped her hands against her phone. "Dominic Grayson filed the missing person report. Took him two days to report her missing, though."

"Two days?" Annie glanced up. "Why the delay?"

Tink skimmed the notes. "Told police he wasn't worried at first. They didn't always talk every day, and they didn't live together. Margot was a woman in her thirties, not a child."

Annie frowned. "Fair enough, what made him contact the police in the end?"

"He said she missed his son's birthday, and that was highly unusual." Tink read from her screen. "It's sad that Margot had no other people in her life."

"Are we sure that's true?" Swift asked.

"No one else came forward?" Annie asked Tink. "That could be enough for the officers back then to write off any other relationships."

"Maybe," Tink nodded. "But surely they would have tried to at least delve into who she spent her time with?"

"Tink, I suggest you and Page go and look into Margot's friends and relationships, see what you can find. There's got to be a link somewhere." Swift stood with a groan, patting the backs of his trouser legs. "Annie, you and I are off to talk to Brannon again. If I sit here any longer I'm going to get piles."

"Do we know how much the transfer was between Brannon and Vivienne?" Annie asked. "The one just before Eliza's death."

"The last transfer?" Tink scrolled on her phone again. "Yep, £500,000."

Swift let out a low breath. "Even for someone as well off as Brannon, that's a lot of money."

"Certainly is." Tink nodded.

"But we don't know what it's for? Or do we?" Annie added.

Page shook his head. "It wasn't part of the official accounts. There are receipts for paintings from his previous purchases, but not this transfer. But the unfinished painting wasn't up for sale from the gallery, or anywhere. Do we think Brannon was willing to pay half a million to get his hands on it?"

"And if so, why?" Tink added. "And how? Would half a million be enough for Vivienne to do away with Eliza to get Brannon the painting?"

A silence settled over them.

"Do you think that Eliza's death and Margot's disappearance are linked?" Annie asked, eventually, breaking through the quiet.

"We've got the missing woman's DNA under our dead woman's fingernails. I'd say so, yes."

"I know that. I'm thinking more than just the DNA, though," Annie went on. "Do you think that the same person who killed Eliza could be involved in Margot's disappearance? They killed Margot to silence her, for whatever reason, and now they've had to do the same to Eliza because she'd started painting her?"

"Possibility." Swift nodded. "Why did Eliza start to paint her after all this time? We can ask the art collector if he knows anything. He's so obsessed with the painting that he might have an idea. And I'd also like to know why he'd been depositing large sums of money into Vivienne's bank account. We'll meet back at the station later. Before we speak again to Dominic Grayson and Clara. I want to go armed with as much information as we can. Clara was the closest person to Eliza, by all accounts, she's got to know more than she's letting on."

When they arrived at the Brannon estate, the art dealer was nowhere to be seen. Instead, they were greeted by a man in a black suit with a white dicky bow. Brannon had a butler? Annie felt like laughing at the absurdity, was it not for the grim reality of the case. The servant led them to Brannon's study where the man himself didn't even deign to turn to greet them. The study was a room filled with floor-to-ceiling bookshelves, leather chairs, and the unmistakable scent of expensive cigars. No artwork though, just a few macabre looking bronzes. Annie studied them closely, her nose wrinkled. A face twisted in agony; a hare still caught in a snare, panic on its face as it struggled to get free. Annie shuddered, wondering if he had chosen this room deliberately.

Brannon stood by the window, a glass of whiskey in hand, looking for all the world like a man who had never worried about a single consequence in his life.

"Detective Swift," he said, finally turning to greet them after the butler had announced them and left the room. "And Miss O'Malley. To what do I owe the pleasure?"

Swift didn't waste time. "We know about the half a million you paid Vivienne Hart. And the small, regular payments you have been making to the gallery."

For a split second, Brannon's hand tightened on the glass. Annie saw the tell-tale white knuckled grip of someone trying to compose themselves.

Then he smirked, taking a slow sip. "That's quite an allegation, Detective."

Swift folded his arms. "It's quite a lot of money. And it's not an allegation, Mr Brannon, it's fact. We have the bank statements."

Brannon let out a low chuckle, shaking his head. "Vivienne and I have a business arrangement."

Annie narrowed her eyes. "You were buying a painting?"

Brannon turned, finally meeting her gaze, his face not hiding his dislike. "I collect art, Miss O'Malley. It's what I do."

"Which painting was it you were buying?" Swift's voice was cold.

Brannon's smirk faltered for the briefest second.

Then he sighed, placing his glass down on a marble-topped side table. "We haven't decided on the artwork."

"What?" Annie pressed.

Brannon exhaled. "It's not out of the ordinary to put down money with a gallery account before an exhibition, it meant I would have first choice from the pieces on display. It's how our relationship works. Not sure how much it will get me now Eliza is no longer with us, mind. I might need to up my budget."

Swift wasn't buying it. "Try again."

Brannon's gaze flickered with something darker. "You wouldn't understand."

"Try me," Annie said, stepping closer.

Brannon studied her for a moment. Then, voice low, he murmured, "no."

A prickle of unease ran down Annie's spine, but she carried on, undeterred. "I've never heard of someone paying half a million pounds to be given first dibs on a painting."

Brannon hesitated. Then, with something almost like reverence, he said, "I don't imagine you would. Our circles are very different. Whereas, to me, that kind of money is available as 'first dibs' money as you so eloquently put it. I think, perhaps, that amount of money might change your life. It's hard to see from my perspective, Annie, when it causes nothing but jealously."

The silence that fell over the room was red hot

and palpable. Annie felt her fists ball and had to shake out her arms to relax them.

"You were hoping the portrait of Margot Grayson would be displayed, weren't you?" Annie's voice was sharp.

"I'm sorry, who?" Brannon scoffed, but Annie could tell he was lying.

"Well you won't be buying any paintings, the exhibition is cancelled," Swift said, and Annie enjoyed watching the blood drain from the collector's face.

"Why are you so invested in having that painting?" Annie went on. "Do you know where it has gone? Did you kill Vivienne Hart, Mr Brannon?"

A wash of panic flashed over Brannon's face.

"What do you mean? Vivienne isn't dead." He baulked.

It was the first time she'd seen him unbalanced.

"Where were you last night? And, actually, where were you Sunday night?" Swift asked.

Brannon smirked, trying to regain the upper hand, but it didn't quite reach his eyes. "At home with my wife. Just like I was the last time you spoke to me. Just like I am every night."

"Is your wife here? Can we verify that?"

"She's indisposed again, she's a busy woman, detective."

Annie folded her arms. "Did you kill Eliza when she wouldn't sell the painting to you? Did you break into her studio and steal it? Or did you go to the gallery in the hope that Vivienne had the painting and then you killed her when you realised she would never be able to get it for you?"

Brannon laughed outright at that. "Please. I don't get my hands dirty. And besides, if I wanted someone dead, you'd never find the body. I am sorry that Vivienne is gone though, she was a good contact for me."

Annie didn't doubt that for a second. But before she could push further about where he might hide a dead body, Swift's phone buzzed sharply in his pocket. He pulled it out, glanced at the screen, and immediately tensed.

"We're done," he said. "For now. An officer will be here shortly to take a formal statement about your whereabouts. Try to raise contact with your wife so she can give her version of events too."

Brannon raised his glass in mock toast. "A pleasure, as always."

Annie stormed from the room, resisting the urge to throw something at Brannon's stupid, smug face.

"Oof, what a horrible man," Annie shook out her body to rid it of the pent up tension as she marched to the car. "What was the message, where are we going?"

"That was Page," Swift said. "They've got a list of artworks from Eliza's will, and they think we're going to want to see it."

TWELVE

THERE WAS NOTHING THEY COULD DO IN THE OFFICE, the noise levels were so high they'd probably be deemed unacceptable under health and safety laws. One of the Traffic Team was turning thirty, but judging by the whoops, cheers, and unmistakable bangs of the party poppers, it looked less like a grown-man's celebration and more like a university frat party.

Annie let the door swing shut behind her and Swift, shaking her head as a burst of off-key singing echoed from inside.

"Where was our invite?" Swift asked as they hurried down the corridor, heading to the incident room instead.

"Lost in the post, thank god," Annie laughed. "I think it's probably a free for all," she added, seeing Swift's face fall.

The incident room was peacefully party free. Page

was sitting at the table, a large folder open in front of him. Tink was on the phone, pacing up and down by the window, her arms flailing around as she spoke in a staccato of angry words.

"Yes, I understand you have procedures, but this is a murder investigation," she said. "No, I don't need a full list of storage policies, I need you to tell me why the hell some of Eliza Warren's archived pieces are missing."

Annie raised an eyebrow at Page as she slid into a chair. "What's she lost?"

Page grimaced. "Not her. Apparently, some of Eliza's older works were sent into long-term storage when we collected them from the crime scene, but now no-one can find half of them."

Swift leaned back in his chair. "Great. Just the ones from the gallery, though, not the ones from her home?"

"Bingo." Page tapped a line on the document in front of him. "Which is good for us right now as here we have a copy of the estate from Eliza Warren's will. Specifically, the list of paintings she left behind that were either on display in her home or already up in the gallery."

Annie and Swift both leaned in.

The pages were dense with legal jargon, asset divisions, and bequests. But in block capitals, starting about half-way down the page was the inventory of artwork—a full catalogue of Eliza's private collection, compiled and sorted by title, date, and location.

It looked like everything was listed here, except the stacks of paintings that Eliza hadn't deemed worthy enough to gift in the event of her death. It should have made things clearer. Instead, it just made things worse.

Annie scanned the list, searching for what could have filled the gap in Eliza's bedroom. The square patch of wallpaper not sun bleached from the window.

"I don't see it." Annie scanned back and forth, seeing all the painting names with small crosses beside them as the forensic team had found and catalogued the artwork. The only one without a cross was the unfinished painting of Margot.

"Hold on," Annie said, face screwed up in confusion. "'Portrait of Margot' was in the studio, why is that on the list of items at Eliza's home? It wasn't even finished."

"Exactly." Page flipped the page and pointed to the tiny, black and white photograph of a portrait that must have been taken when the will was written up.

Swift frowned. "What are we looking at?"

Page exhaled. "A painting titled 'Portrait of Margot.'"

Annie's brain hurt.

"I can't see it clearly," Swift asked, his voice edged with something unreadable. "But this photo looks old. Which doesn't make sense."

"It is old," Page said. "It's weird. This was catalogued as part of Eliza's estate as one of the early paintings. It's been hanging on her bedroom wall for over twenty years."

Annie's pulse kicked up a notch. "You mean the one stolen from the studio?"

Page nodded. "Yep. That's what doesn't make sense." He flipped back a few pages. "The portrait listed in the will. It was completed years ago. It's written up as a finished piece, with date and everything."

Annie frowned. "But the one we saw in the studio wasn't finished. I wish this photo was better quality. Can't even zoom in."

"Exactly." Page leaned back, rubbing his jaw. "Maybe Eliza painted two versions of Margot Grayson and the painting that was stolen wasn't the one she originally left behind."

Annie exchanged a look with Swift. There was something niggling at her brain, but she wasn't yet able to put a name on it.

"But if there are two," Swift said slowly, "Where the hell have they both gone?"

"That's why Tink is giving storage a piece of her mind," Page replied, as Tink growled like an angry cat across the room. "She's checking to see if we collected the one from Eliza's bedroom before it was added to the evidence list."

Annie shook her head, thinking to herself that if that was the case, then why was it already missing from the bedroom when she was at the house, when none of the other paintings had been taken?

Tink returned, dropping her phone onto her desk with an irritated sigh. "Storage is a mess. They can't find half the evidence they should have down there. Apparently, there's a new cataloguing system in place that uses AI to organise it and now the whole basement facility has come to a standstill."

"That's what we get for letting computers take over the world," Annie shrugged. "They'll be sliding up the stairs to join the Traffic party if we're not careful."

Swift smiled and Tink came to sit with them, dejectedly throwing herself onto a chair.

"It might not even be down there," Annie added.

Tink nodded. "You're right. How did you get on with Brannon?"

Annie's stomach coiled in memory at the arrogant dealer and the way he'd dismissed her because she was a woman who didn't have half a million in spare change.

"He's hiding something." Annie chewed the inside of her cheek. "There's no way he paid Vivienne that much money just in case there was something he wanted in the exhibition. It doesn't work like that."

"I've asked the forensic accountants to look deeper into Vivienne's bank accounts," Swift said. "And Eliza's too. I'm sure it's no coincidence that there was a large sum paid to Vivienne from the artist just before she died."

The DI turned to the whiteboard and sighed. It was a mess of pictures and names and arrows. Still too many question marks littered the case, and Annie felt like it was too hard to see the woods for the trees. Two deaths, Eliza and Vivienne. A missing person, Margot. An angry art dealer with more money than taste. Margot's brother, Dominic. Eliza's assistant, Clara. Not to mention money changing hands like sweets. What was going on?

"What about you guys," Annie asked, turning back to Page. "Did you manage to gather anything about Margot's friends or boyfriends or girlfriends?"

"Not a lot," the DS replied, rubbing his temples. "We dug through old reports, press clippings, and police notes from when Margot went missing. No close friends came forward. No lovers that were found. A very brief statement from Eliza and a longer one from Dominic, but nothing of substance to tell us who Margot really was."

Swift's jaw tensed. "Meaning she was keeping secrets. Why have a MisPer file if there's no-one who's missing you? There must have been someone else."

"Do we know what she did for a job?" Annie asked.

"She was an artist too," Page said, surprising Annie that this hadn't been discussed before. "At least, she was trying her very best to be an artist. It's harder when you come from a background like Margot and Dominic."

"What kind of background?" Swift asked.

"Working class," Page replied. "No disposable income."

"I wonder if Margot was trying to discard her old life and make a new one for herself," Annie said. "Maybe that's why she didn't have a lot of people around her? Maybe she turned her back on them, rather than the other way around."

"Interesting idea, Annie," Swift said, nodding. "Did the old case files delve further back into Margot's life?"

"Just what Dominic told the officers at the time," Tink piped up. "Nothing that stood out."

Annie exhaled slowly. Margot must have been surrounded by people in the art world—artists, collectors, gallery owners, dealers. And yet, despite all of that, she had vanished without a trace. Maybe she was so new into the world that nobody cared. Or maybe she was recognised as an outsider, and nobody wanted to be tarred with that brush.

Tink was scanning her notes, flicking through a thin stack of old case summaries. "We found a few acquaintances who said Margot and Eliza knew each other professionally. Apparently, they met through the art scene. Margot had worked on a few restoration projects, and Eliza had been involved in some of the same circles."

Annie frowned. "But no record of them being particularly close?"

Page shook his head. "Nothing solid. No evidence

that they were friends. But there's something else. We found an address."

Annie leaned in. "An address for what?"

Page slid a grainy black-and-white printout of the last photograph taken of Margot across the table. He added another picture on top. This one was the outside of a building, short and squat like a turtle. "The address of the last place Margot was seen. The party where that photo was taken."

Annie's pulse skipped as she pulled the photo towards her. She didn't recognise the building.

"Where is this? Is it local?"

"No, London." Page flipped another sheet of paper over to Annie and Swift's side of the table. "The address used to be a hip and trendy warehouse back in the nineties. Not sure what it is now, I'm just doing a search for it on land registry, won't take long."

He pulled his laptop closer and thumbed at the mousepad, sucking at his teeth as he did so. Annie and Swift poured over the photograph of the outside of the building. If Page was right, and this unimaginative, stark looking building was part of a trendy scene, then Annie could understand why she had never been part of that scene herself. She preferred comfort over making a statement.

"Oh." Page let out a long, low whistle.

"What?" Swift leaned in to the DS's screen, eyes squinted like he needed glasses but wasn't giving in to the notion.

"The warehouse was razed to the ground and is now a lovely block of flats!" Annie heard the sarcasm in his voice. "But it *was* owned by none other than our friend, Mr Dominic Grayson."

A slow, uneasy silence settled over the room as the news sank in.

"So Margot disappeared from a place owned by her own brother," Tink said. "How was that missed during the initial investigation? No one thought that was important enough to look into back then?"

Page smirked, but it was humourless. "Seems like a massive oversight, doesn't it? But let's give the officers credit, it was easier to list assets under companies back then, with no ties to real names. It wasn't until 2018 when the new GDPR laws came in that Grayson's name was even attached to it, and he sold it to a developer for a cool three million in the same year she went missing."

Annie's mind was racing. Dominic had reported Margot missing. He had insisted she wasn't the type to disappear. But now, suddenly, he was connected to the very last place she had been seen alive?

If Dominic had nothing to hide then why had he never mentioned it?

"Right," Swift was a man on a mission. He clapped his hands and stood so purposefully that Annie thought his back might need a once over from a chiropractor. "Annie, you and I are off to find out why Grayson omitted a rather important piece of information. Page, Tink, you guys need to go and speak to

Clara again, can you try and find out if Eliza and Dominic knew each other better than Dominic is letting on. And ask again if Clara has any idea about the painting of Margot that was in Eliza's bedroom and where the bloody hell that one has gone. Tink, am I boring you?"

All eyes fell on Tink who was, from looking at her, ignoring Swift and engrossed in her phone screen. Her brows shot up and she shook her head.

"No, guv, well, not this time, anyway." She grinned. "But sometimes, yeah, when you start to—"

Swift gave a pointed cough.

"Fair enough," Tink said in reply. "But we've just had an anonymous tip off that one of the missing paintings is about to go up for auction. Small auction place in Essex."

"What?" Swift baulked. "Get on it. You can go and pick it up yourself, Tink. Page, you'll be okay talking to Clara alone. With any luck, that painting will hold all the answers we need."

THIRTEEN

Tink had never really liked auction houses. Not that she'd been in many, and certainly not any in her adulthood. Her mum and dad had dragged her to a few growing up, their house stuffed to the rafters with old tat. Or objet d'art as they called it. Walking up to the old barn housing The Montford Auction House, in the middle-of-nowhere, Essex, Tink could just picture her dad in his tweed cap and her mum in her pearls and made a mental note to invite them over for dinner when the case was solved and she had the spare time to roast a lamb with rosemary sprigs and proper gravy.

She brushed down her bright yellow jacket and headed for the front door, hoping that the clientele had changed since she'd last been to a show. It wasn't the art that Tink didn't like, that part she got. The paintings, the sculptures, the antiques. She could appreciate the history and the craftsmanship. It was the people that got under her skin. The less-than-subtle once over from onlookers. Are you wearing the right clothes? Does your bag cost more than a couple of months' wages? Are your jewels real? Even though most of the time they were all huddled together in an old, dusty cattle shed, if you weren't one of them, you were elbowed to the back of the room and shunned. Tink's parents wore the right clothes, but somehow the old money could smell the desperation from the charity shop Mulberry Bags and the holy Burberry scarves. When Tink was old enough, she'd decided to go against the grain and wear what she loved and not what she thought would impress others. Because she'd seen first-hand that it didn't work.

"Hello?" She pushed on the door, despite the closed sign.

It squeaked on its hinges and juddered to a halt half-way open. Squeezing inside, Tink smelt the musty scent of antiques and something faintly chemical and was thrown right back to being an awkward fifteen-year-old. She headed for the rows of auction items out on display and reminded herself that she was a police officer who was very good at her job.

"Hello," she called again, stepping between a walnut cabinet and the back of a Victorian looking armchair.

Accoutrement littered the surfaces of all the chests and cabinets. Small snuff boxes hidden beside vases probably worth more than Tink's car. She fought the urge to nudge a glass decanter off the edge of a tall boy with her pinky finger and listen to it smash on the bare concrete floor. But maybe she wasn't doing a good job of hiding her compulsion because a voice rang out softly through the large space.

"Can I help you?"

Tink peered around, trying to find the owner of the voice, but the room looked empty of people. A shuffle of movement and a head peered around the wings of the armchair right beside her. Tink started, a hand rushing to her chest.

"Christ on a bike," she yelled. "You made me jump."

The voice belonged to a man. Tink guessed at around her age, mid to late twenties. He had rolled-up sleeves, tailored trousers, light brown hair slightly too mussed for someone in this line of work. His chestnut eyes twinkled with mischief and Tink saw right away that he did have auctioneer written all over him. Polished, professional, the kind of man who could charm a fortune out of a collector with nothing but a raised eyebrow. The kind of man who could charm *her* with nothing but a raised eyebrow.

"We're closed." He stood, offering his hand.

Nothing about what he'd just said made Tink think he was commanding her to leave. Quite the opposite, if anything. She took his hand and shook it, their eyes stuck for a beat on each other.

Tink remembered why she was there and tried to gain some semblance of authority. She reached for her bag and flashed her badge, holding out a printed photo of the painting to the man. He took it, brushing Tink's fingers with his own.

"This painting," she nodded to the photo, trying to ignore the man's advances, which was hard as he was very cute. "Was stolen from a crime scene. I have reason to believe you've got it up for auction."

The man got to his feet.

Oh man, Tink's resolve was flying out the window as he stood at least six foot.

"Well then, officer," he said, smiling. "I'd be a fool not to help you."

She nodded. "Yes, yes you would, Mr…"

"Harebelle." He cocked his head. "But you can call me Ben, officer."

"DS Lock." Tink motioned to the photograph again. "What can you tell me about this painting?"

"Come with me," Ben replied, edging past her with a waft of something expensive.

They weaved through the larger pieces of furniture, a rather stunning mid-century coffee table catching Tink's eye on the way, until they were deep at the back of the auction house where stacks of paintings leant against the drywall covering.

And there it was. Resting against a few other paintings, still wrapped in protective sheeting, was Eliza Warren's unfinished portrait.

Tink stepped forward, recognising it immediately as the portrait that had gone missing from the studio break in. She'd not particularly warmed to it from the crime scene photos, but the way Annie had described it had seemed a little far-fetched. Now, up close, Tink knew exactly what her friend had meant. Her hackles rose and she felt her nose tickle. Even half-finished and wrapped in plastic, the woman in the painting looked like she was watching and waiting for Tink to make a mistake. Margot Grayson, incomplete but as haunting as ever.

A whisper of unease crawled down the back of Tink's neck and she span around to see who was there and what was causing it. But the auctioneer was the only one around.

"Everything okay?" Ben asked, a sincere look of concern on his face.

"Do you not find this creepy?" she murmured, before coming to her senses. "Look, this is evidence in a murder, I'm going to need to take it with me."

"Don't you need a warrant to do that?" Ben asked, a lilt of amusement on his words.

Tink pulled on a pair of blue gloves from her pocket and wrapped her fingers around the top of the frame, heaving it up and over the pile of records on the floor. It was heavier than she'd expected it to be and her arms shook with the angle and the weight. Ben's hands shot out and helped her gently lower it to the floor by their feet. She saw he was wearing white, cotton gloves and weirdly they didn't give her the ick.

"I'm not sure I can just hand it over," Ben said, warily now.

"I'm going to need details of who's selling it too,

name, contact number, address if you have it." Tink narrowed her eyes.

"I'll need to check about handing out personal details," he replied, again, trying to push the point.

"We've got an active crime," Tink added. "And currently, you're handling stolen goods. So you can give me the information, or I can speak to your boss about where we go from here."

The corner of Ben's mouth lifted. "I am the boss. This is my place."

"Oh, right." Tink felt her cheeks heat. "In that case, you should probably give me the requested information, or I might have to shut down the whole building and wait for a warrant. What's your preference?"

Ben raised a brow. It wasn't really a question that needed answering.

"I'll take your word for it that giving out private information isn't illegal or against GDPR regulations, Officer Lock." Ben ran a hand through his hair. "But I'm going to need your name and number, you know, just in case it ever comes up."

Tink laughed. "Nice try."

Ben grinned, head cocked like he knew she had the willpower of a gnat when it came to cute men.

"Come on then, my office is this way," he said, turning. "I'll have the information you're looking for on file."

Ben's office wasn't really an office, it was a stable at the other end of the barn conversion. With a half door and a horseshoe still hung overhead, it felt like something out of a Western.

"Good luck?" Tink asked, nodding at the horseshoe.

"It was my pony's," Ben said, almost embarrassed. "Used to live in here before my parents converted half their farm into an auction house."

"Cute," Tink replied. "Did he have to get rehomed when his stable became your office, or do you share?"

It was Ben's turn to laugh. "He was just moved to the other stable block, but he's long gone now. RIP Pickles."

Ben opened the half-door and a shaggy sheepdog lolloped to his heels.

"You sure it's not still a farm?" Tink asked, giving the dog's head a tickle.

"Meet Digby," Ben said, sitting down at the old writing desk and firing up an ancient computer. "He was in training to be my parents' next working collie, but he kept trying to befriend the sheep by licking their faces, so he's mine now."

Tink felt his soft fur and the warmth of his head through her fingers.

"Licking faces is not how to make friends, Digby."

"Oh," Ben said, typing away. "Isn't it? That must be where I'm going wrong."

He looked over at Tink with a mischievous glint in his eyes.

"That's weird," Ben said, his attention back on his computer.

"What?" Tink moved closer, trying to get a look at the screen.

"There doesn't seem be any record of this painting." Ben started typing again, moving the mouse and clicking furiously "Nope, nothing. I don't even know how it ended up in the stack to be honest, it's not even in the catalogue for this evening's auction."

"Then how did someone get an anonymous tip off to us that it was going up for sale?"

"Sorry, Officer, I can't answer that." Ben stood up again and Digby stayed by his heels.

"Any CCTV?" Tink asked, but Ben shook his head. "Eliza Warren, do you know her?"

"I've heard the name, sadly never been lucky enough to have one of her pieces for sale here. Hold, on, is that a Warren?" Ben asked, eyeing the painting that Tink had leant against the doorframe.

"It is, yes. Do you know an Edward Brannon or a Margot Grayson?"

Ben shook his head. 'Not that I can think of, no. You mean to tell me that I had a Warren here in my auction house and I didn't even know it? Wow... wait, did you say this was a murder enquiry?"

"Yes, sadly Eliza Warren was found dead in her studio a couple of nights ago, and the gallery owner, Vivienne Hart was found dead in her gallery not long after."

"Urgh, do you think I need to watch my back?"

Ben asked, grimacing. "Do you want to provide me with a round-the-clock police guard?"

"No." Tink picked up the painting and started for the door.

"Are you sure, you look like you're thinking about it," Ben called after her. "Hesitating a little."

"I'm not hesitating," Tink said, squeezing herself and the portrait through the jammed doorway. "I'm thinking about whether or not to arrest you for handling stolen goods."

He grinned. "And what have you decided?"

"You're lucky I have places to be."

His voice followed her as she walked away. "Shame."

Tink refused to acknowledge the flicker of amusement in her chest as she climbed into her yellow Punto and strapped the portrait into the passenger seat beside her. She patted it to make sure it was safe, and a card fell from the plastic wrapping. Picking it up she saw Ben's name and number scrawled neatly on the back of the auction house business card. Tink put it in her glovebox for safe keeping, in case she needed it for a follow up work call.

You're kidding no-one, Tink!

She put the car into first gear and headed on her way back to Norfolk, whistling a happy tune. But it wasn't long before her whistles grew quieter and the car grew smaller. Something wasn't right. Her head felt off. Like pressure behind her eyes, a slow, dull ache curling at the base of her skull. Not a migraine, not quite. She rolled her shoulders, fingers gripping the wheel a little too tight. She was normally quite good at ignoring things. Uncomfortable truths. Bad memories. The feeling that something was watching her from the passenger seat.

Tink turned her head, but the painting was just as she'd left it. She flicked the radio on. The signal crackled, then died.

She exhaled, shaking her head. "Brilliant."

The back of her neck itched. The headache throbbed, spreading slow and heavy, making her temples pulse and igniting a creeping sensation that someone was sitting close behind her.

She glanced in the rearview mirror, but the back seats were empty.

It was stupid. For a second, she could have sworn she saw movement to her left. It must have been just a trick of the light.

Then she heard a whisper. So soft she almost thought she imagined it.

"Look."

She pressed her foot to the accelerator, ignoring the way her skin prickled with something she refused to name. It was just a painting. Just a piece of stretched canvas and oil paint.

So why did it feel like it was alive?

FOURTEEN

Dominic Grayson lived well. Annie could tell the second she stepped out of the car. He lived in a suburb just outside of the city, a new build home in an exclusive gated community where they had privacy, warmth, and more than one en-suite. His gravel was raked to within an inch of its life and Annie wondered if there was a separate entrance for use and this one was just for show.

Swift shut his door and shuffled his feet a little, rucking up the stones beneath them with a grin on his face.

"Oops," he said. "Silly me."

They peered at the windows, and Annie half expected to see Grayson bound out the door, rake in hand, to rectify Swift's mischief. But the house stayed quiet.

"Nice place for someone who spent half our last

conversation acting like a struggling sibling of a missing person."

"People grieve in different ways," Annie replied, stepping up to the door. "Apparently, Grayson's way was turning a profit on the building where his sister was last seen."

She rang the bell. Somewhere inside, a chime echoed, low and melodic. After a pause, the door opened.

Dominic Grayson stood there, still as sharp as the last time they'd seen him. No pocket square today, but he was dressed in a tailored navy jumper and chinos. If grief had ever hollowed him out, there was no trace of it on his face.

"Detectives," he said smoothly, stepping back to let them in.

His house was as expensive inside as it was out. Muted greys, expensive looking furniture, a curated sort of wealth. Not cluttered, but deliberate; like a show home that someone happened to live in. Annie scanned the walls, noticing the absence of something. No photographs of Margot. No reminder that she ever existed. Though there were no photos of anyone, so perhaps Dominic didn't like to display his life for guests to see.

They went to the living room and Dominic gestured toward the sleek, modern sofa. "I assume this isn't a social visit?"

Swift settled into the chair opposite, ignoring

Dominic's offer. "Let's talk about the last place Margot was seen."

For a fraction of a second, Dominic stilled. His jaw tightened and his eyes wrinkled into a scowl.

"I already told you—"

"You told us," Annie interrupted, "that Margot wasn't the type to disappear. That you were the one who reported her missing." She sat down on the sofa. "What you didn't tell us was that she disappeared from a building you owned at the time."

There was a stilted silence in the room, thick, like a fog.

Dominic crossed his arms over his chest, his fingers tapped lightly on his elbows.

"I don't see why that's relevant." He stayed standing.

Annie scoffed. "Seriously?"

Swift's voice was sharper. "You don't think it's relevant that your sister was last seen at your property, at your event, and you conveniently forgot to mention that detail? Did you mention it to the officers at the time?"

Dominic's lips pressed together, his composure holding—but just barely. "I assume that the officers at the time would have done their due diligence and seen that I used to own the old warehouse, yes. And I didn't mention it to you, because it had nothing to do with what happened to her. And you're not investigating my sister's disappearance, are you?"

Annie shook her head, her brows knotted. "It's still pertinent information, Mr Grayson,"

There was a long pause, then, finally, he sighed, shifting slightly, his chin dropping as though deciding on something.

"It was my warehouse, but it wasn't actually my event," he said. "I used to hire out the space. In actual fact, I originally bought the warehouse for Margot so she could turn it into a studio, back when we both lived in London. I felt bad for her, you understand. Our parents had paid to send me to a fantastic school, I was lucky. But when Margot came along a lot later—a surprise if you will—I was away at university so our parents had kind of semi-retired and there was no money left in the pot. I felt like I had all the advantages. Good schooling. A Cambridge degree. A job in finance. I wanted to give Margot the same foot up that I'd had, just a little later on in her life."

Swift frowned. "That's very generous of you, Mr Grayson."

"I worked in The City." Dominic cut in. "I made ridiculous amounts of money, and it was the least I could do for Margot who had been back here in Norfolk caring for our elderly parents since leaving high school. I wanted her to come to London, to live the life she wanted for herself. She was naturally talented and could have been a great artist. But, with hindsight, I wish I'd just left her alone. None of this would have happened if I'd left her alone."

"None of this?" Annie asked, skin prickling. She glanced at Swift, who was already leaning forward.

"Yes." Dominic sounded impatient. "This. Her going missing, not having a life at all, let alone a life in London. And you two turning up in my life twenty years later, hounding me about something that makes me feel guilt every single day. Our parents died of broken hearts within a year of Margot going missing. I think they blamed me too."

"Do you think the death of Eliza has anything to do with the disappearance of Margot?" Annie asked, trying to solidify any firm attachments between the two. "Can you think of any idea why Eliza had started painting your sister again, after all these years?"

Dominic looked like a man beaten. His shell was crumbling around him and Annie realised that what she'd said at the door was truer than ever. People really did grieve in different ways. Outwardly he had been a successful businessman, but inside Dominic had been blaming himself all these years and it had taken its toll.

"I honestly don't know."

"You said that Eliza and Margot got on okay, were friends, even?" Annie asked. "Do you know if Margot commissioned the original painting of herself or was it just a portrait between friends?"

Eliza had kept that portrait in her bedroom, perhaps Margot was more than just a friend?

"Look, in all honesty, I wasn't too keen on the crowd that Margot had instilled herself amongst."

Dominic straightened his sleeves. "They were a hippy lot, free love and all of that nonsense. A lot of them were a good ten, twenty years older than Margot, but they were still running around like children, the lot of them. But then there wasn't a lot I could say to Margot, seeing as it was my fault she was in the City to start with. She found an adventurous side when she moved up there and I found out that parenting a young woman, even in her early thirties who had just found freedom, wasn't easy, especially as I wasn't a parent, I was just a sibling."

"Margot was her own woman. She was an adult." Annie wasn't going to tell Dominic that he'd done his best, she had no idea if he had protected Margot or left her to her own devices. But a little bit of truth wouldn't hurt. Margot had been in her thirties, she wasn't a child.

"Let's go back to this warehouse for a moment" Swift said, sitting back in his chair and crossing his ankles. "Did Margot use it for what you hoped she would? Was she working as an artist there? Maybe letting the other artists use the space too?"

Annie could see the cogs turning behind Swift's eyes and she wished she knew what had sparked the line of questioning. She wracked her brains to what Grayson had already said but nothing sprang to mind.

"In a way, I guess she was," Dominic replied. "They'd use the space for shows, though, rather than working. It was a bit dark, perhaps, to make a good studio. I can see that now I have an idea of how artists like to work. But it made a terrific venue for shows and parties and gatherings of the sort Margot liked to attend."

A little light flashed on in Annie's mind, she stowed away her question for when Swift had finished his.

"And what made you sell up?" Swift added when Dominic had finished.

"I…" a flash of emotion poured over Dominic and a small tear fell down his reddened cheeks. "There was no point in keeping it when the one person I'd bought it for wasn't there to use it."

Dominic's fingers curled against his arms. Annie wished he'd sit down, if nothing else she was worried about him keeling over. He was giving all the right answers to convince them that he had nothing to do with the disappearance of his sister, but he had had twenty years to practise.

"I don't know what happened to her," Dominic added, voice clipped. "But I know she didn't just leave that night. I knew it then, and I know it now."

Annie looked to Swift, questioningly, and he gave her the nod to go ahead.

"Mr Grayson, Dominic," Annie said. "Do you think Eliza could have had something to do with Margot's disappearance? A lover's tiff, perhaps."

If Dominic disliked the idea of Margot being in a relationship with a woman, he did nothing to show it.

"No, I don't think that's the case." He shook his head. "Margot was definitely straight. In fact, I think she was seeing one of the boys who regularly held events in the warehouse. Many of them, in fact."

Annie wasn't sure if he meant many events or many boys, but she didn't take that route.

"And you said before that the event Margot went missing at wasn't one of your own, is that right?"

Dominic nodded, a crease between his brows. "Yes."

"Do you remember what kind of event it was?" she asked.

"That night is forever etched on my memory. Though I wasn't there, I have seen enough CCTV footage and photographic evidence to never be able to forget. It was an exhibition."

"An art exhibition?"

"Yes, run by an up and coming collector."

"Do you remember who?"

"Of course." Dominic exhaled sharply, shaking his head. "The same person Margot was supposedly seeing, though I think he was seeing other people too as she was very hush hush about it when I asked."

He met Annie's gaze, and she knew, instinctively, that whatever he was about to say would change everything.

"What was his name?" she whispered.

"Oh, just some guy called Edward." Dominic looked out of the window into the dying light. "I only remember as he was the one who bought the warehouse from me. I thought maybe he would keep it as a place in Margot's memory, a place where artists could work and exhibit for free. It's not like he was short of a bob or two. But he raised the warehouse to the ground, pretty much immediately after buying it. It's a block of flats now, and not even affordable ones at that. Though I suppose that's what you get in the centre of London."

"Edward?" Annie prompted, though she was sure she knew the man's surname already.

"Edward Brannon."

Annie felt her stomach plunge. Brannon. Edward Brannon. Not just a patron of the arts. Not just an over-invested collector. But a man very much entwined in Eliza and Margot's lives.

Swift swore under his breath. "So Brannon was seeing the young Margot and then reduced to rubble her last known whereabouts? I can't imagine his wife was too pleased about that."

Dominic nodded stiffly. "I should have—" He cut himself off, scrubbing a hand down his face. "I wish I'd kept the warehouse myself. Edward Brannon couldn't have cared less about Margot, let alone a building bought in her honour."

Annie's head buzzed with the weight of it.

Brannon had positioned himself so carefully in all of this. But this changed things. Brannon had been at the event where Margot had disappeared. He'd been desperate to buy the portrait of Margot. And he'd had the opportunity to kill both Eliza and Vivienne. And he'd bought the last place Margot had been seen.

Swift's voice was tight with frustration. "Why the hell didn't you mention this before?"

Dominic met his gaze, and for the first time, something raw and vulnerable cut through his mask.

"I didn't think it was relevant," he admitted. "Why would a London developer have anything to do with the death of an artist? You were investigating that, looking into the woman who painted my sister, it just didn't register."

Annie understood what he meant, and she shook her head almost imperceptibly at Swift who looked like he was about to blow a gasket.

Annie stood, thanking Mr Grayson, and heading out of the room.

"This just put Brannon at the top of our list," she said to Swift.

"Firmly." Swift held out a hand to Grayson.

Dominic let out a long breath, something like relief and regret tangled together and shook Swift's hand. As they reached the front door, Annie turned back.

"I'm sorry that your sister has never been found," she offered. "If we get any news that might help reignite her case, I want you to know that we will act on it."

Dominic's face clouded. "I think I'd rather just forget about any of it. What's the use in dredging up old pain? Goodbye detectives."

FIFTEEN

Swift pulled out of Dominic Grayson's pristine driveway with a little more force than necessary. The gravel crunching under the tyres, probably doing more damage than their feet had earlier. Annie felt a pang of guilt at how childish they'd been. Dominic was carrying a lot more than the pain of a missing sister; he had pretty much told them he felt responsible for the fact Margot had vanished. Twenty years of burden he'd been carrying. Perhaps he found comfort in having control over the little things like his driveway gravel, as the big things were so out of reach. No wonder he'd been so quick to say goodbye.

She stared out the window into the dusky purple sky, her thoughts tangled up in what they'd just uncovered. Brannon: the piece of the puzzle that connected Eliza and Vivienne and the subject of Eliza's portrait. Edward Brannon might have been in a relationship with Margot. He had bought the building where Margot was last seen. Had hounded Eliza to buy the portrait of Margot. How had he managed to keep himself out of the investigation into Margot's disappearance back then?

"Okay, so Eliza knew Margot back when she went missing, then," Annie pondered aloud. She found it useful to talk about all of the strands of the case, even if no one was listening. The act of saying it sometimes made pieces of the puzzle become clearer, or slot into the correct place. And Swift was always a good sounding board for those times she wasn't alone, like now. "The disappearance of Eliza's portraits of Margot have to be linked with both Margot's disappearance and with Eliza's death."

"And Vivienne?" Swift asked, flicking the heat on in the car. "Wrong place, wrong time?"

"I don't know," Annie replied. "Maybe. Wrong place and time for what, though? If she knew about what happened to Margot then it's twenty years too late to be bumping her off for it. And the portraits weren't even in her exhibition."

"Vivienne told us she'd accidentally picked up the painting mistaking it for an exhibition piece. And we have an email trail of Eliza asking Vivienne to destroy something for her. Probably the portraits. I wonder if Tink had any luck picking up the one that was called in." Swift flicked a button on the steering wheel and dialled the DS. It rang twice before she picked up.

"MCU's finest, hold on," she greeted, her voice rattled by what sounded like Kansas mid-tornado.

Annie could hear the sound of a car window being lifted and the calm that came when it closed. "How can I help?"

Swift cut to the chase. "Tell me you've got it. And if you do, I hope you have it strapped down tightly because you sound like you're speeding with the windows down."

"Oh, I've got it," she said. "Our very own stolen masterpiece. And it's wrapped up safely next to me, though I was only doing 65 mph." Her voice wavered and Annie knew exactly why. She wouldn't want to be confined to a Punto with unfinished Margot, either.

"In a 30?" Swift asked and Tink uttered a few expletives back.

"It was wrapped up like a crime scene and shoved into the back of a cute little auction house. You'd have loved it, guv—old furniture, probably a cursed object or two, cute doggo. Annie, you'd have loved the auctioneer. Looked a little like a grown-up version of the man in *To All The Boys I've Loved Before*."

Annie smirked. "Noah Centineo? I love him."

"Highlight of my day," Tink said dreamily. "His name's Ben Harebell, lush right?"

"Right," Swift boomed. "And that's important to the case how?"

"Staff wellbeing, boss," Tink quipped back. "Anyway, what am I doing with this ghastly thing, other than trying not to punch it in the eye holes?"

"Can you take it straight to forensics? See if anyone in the lab can get prints or blood or any sort of

DNA that will give us a head start that we're desperate for." Swift moved his hand to hang up before adding. "Then can you go give Page a call? I want us all back at the station for a full debrief."

Tink made a noise of agreement. "On it. He's still at the studio, right?"

"Think so," Annie replied. "He was meeting Clara there. Well, in the cafe downstairs. I've tried calling but he must be mid-interview."

"Just ask that he comes straight back, if you can?" Swift added. "We've got some rather interesting intel on Brannon. All we need is some physical evidence and we can bring him in."

"Great," Tink said. "I'll be there in twenty and I'll head to the incident room after the lab. Toodleoo."

Swift ended the call and focused on the road, but Annie could tell he was still chewing over everything they'd learned. They travelled back to the station in silence, the radio quietly providing a backdrop to Annie's overworking brain.

Rose greeted her friends with a wave as they walked through reception. She held up a hand, seemingly remembering something.

"Hey, guys," she called over to them. "Tink said could you head straight to the lab when you get in?"

They headed over to the reception desk so they didn't have to shout across the entrance hall where a few people were sitting on the plastic seats waiting to be seen.

'Did she say why?" Swift asked.

Rose shook her head. "Nope, just that they had something to show you. Must have been quick work though, Tink's only just back herself."

They gave their thanks and headed on in to the inner sanctum, turning left instead of going to the office or the incident room. The forensic rooms, much like Evans' pathology labs, were stark and bright and didn't hold any traces of stale coffee or musty paper. It was rare that Annie and Swift ventured to this side of the building, mostly they were sent reports via email, so it was a treat for the senses as well as a chance to nosy around.

"Look, Joe," Annie said, pointing through a door to a kitchen. "They've got a Nespresso. Where's our Nespresso?"

"Rude." Swift raised a brow and stuck his head through the door. "You do not want to see what else they've got in here."

"What?" Annie tried to see past him, but his shoulders were in the way.

"An air fryer and a dishwasher." Shaking his head like he couldn't believe what he was seeing.

"I'm staging a rebellion."

"Right after we see what Tink wants," Swift tagged on to the end of Annie's sentence.

"Yes, boss."

They headed through to the sterile brightness of

the forensic lab, where Tink was pacing, phone held to her ear. She held up a finger as she left a voice message seemingly to Page then hung up and took a breath.

"You're never going to guess what they've found?" she said, smiling.

Dr. Lena Dorsey, the lead forensic analyst, stood by a large, flat-screen display, her expression pained. Her hair was tied back in a perfect blonde ponytail and her lab coat was starched white. Annie tugged at the sleeves of her rain Mac and blew out her cheeks, tugging her own wayward hair back up into a messy bun.

The unfinished portrait of Margot was propped up behind Lena, as ghastly as Annie remembered. Margot's ghostly, half-painted face glaring at her from under the harsh lab lighting.

Lena adjusted her glasses, clearing her throat. "DS Lock said you were after DNA and prints."

It took Annie a minute to realise Lena was talking about Tink.

"We'll get around to those as soon as we can," Lena went on. "But when I put the portrait under the UV lights, something weird happened. It was almost as though another figure was looking back at me."

Cogs turned in Annie's brain, clicking into place as Lena continued talking.

"We conducted an X-ray fluorescence scan on the painting, as well as multi-layer imaging. Eliza Warren used traditional oil techniques, meaning each layer can be distinguished separately."

Annie's fingers curled, her nails digging into her palms. "And?"

Lena exhaled, pressing a few keys on the laptop beside her. The screen shifted, the bright colours of the visible painting dissolving into ghostly layers beneath.

Annie's breath hitched. Because Margot's face had changed. The unfinished painting was gone, replaced by something raw and haunting and complete. Margot wasn't just staring out from the canvas. She was afraid. Her eyes wide and terrified. Her body told a different story, too. Dark smudges lined her wrists and upper arms, her eye sockets and cheek bones, barely visible but unmistakable as bruises.

Annie's stomach twisted. Eliza hadn't painted Margot as a muse. She had painted her as a victim.

Swift swore under his breath as Lena gestured to the screen. "The layers show that Eliza originally painted Margot this way, with fear in her eyes and bruises. The portrait you see in front of you is in the process of being altered, it seems as though the artist was trying to remove the bruises and she was in the middle of redoing the expression when she died."

Annie's voice was hoarse; she cleared her throat and felt a sharp pain shoot through her skull.

"Do you think Eliza was painting a new picture to

replace the one that had been taken down from her bedroom?" Tink asked, chewing the inside of her cheek. "Maybe she started painting it exactly the same and then changed her mind about what Margot looked like. Maybe she didn't want to remember her as a victim of whatever caused this." Tink waved at the painting on the screen which showed the marks of someone recently beaten. She then waved her hand to her face. "Do you not have air con in here? You look like you should have, given how high tech this place is. But it's boiling."

Lena agreed, her own face had a faint sheen. Annie coughed again, her head pounding, but she could think straight enough for the answer to one large question to start to become clear.

"I don't think Eliza started again," she said. "I think the painting in Eliza's bedroom and the painting from the studio are the same. Look at the faded paint on the layers underneath, just like the walls had faded around it because of the sun. Eliza took it out of her room herself."

Swift's brows shot into his hairline. "Oh my god, genius," he said. "But why change it now?"

Tink hesitated. "Maybe because she regretted showing the truth. Maybe because she was afraid. Or maybe because someone forced her to."

Annie exhaled, staring at the haunting X-ray image. The hidden Margot. Or maybe just the real Margot. For so long, Margot had been a missing person. A mystery. A name tied to an unsolved disappearance. And Eliza had to have known more than she was letting on, and now they knew what she had been trying to tell them all along. And they knew why someone had wanted her to disappear.

Swift's voice was low. "Eliza hadn't just painted a portrait." He met Annie's gaze. "She had told a story."

"A story that got her killed?" Annie concluded.

"A story that someone is trying to change." Swift span on his heels. "We need to get back to the studio. I have a feeling that there was something else the killer was looking for and I'm not sure they'll stop looking until they have it."

SIXTEEN

ANNIE AND SWIFT PULLED UP AT THE BARN, headlights illuminating the flint work. Tink wasn't far behind, her yellow Punto sliding in beside Swift's 4x4. Night had fallen in its entirety and the hillside was pitch black around the edges of the car lights. Out in the sticks, night seemed more present than in the centre of the city.

"Still no word from Page," Tink said, groaning as she got out. "He might still be interviewing Clara, but that would be the world's longest chat."

"You're too young to be moaning about your joints," Annie noted. "Page is probably raiding the closed kitchen of the cafe. Especially if they have those little individually wrapped cakes. I wonder if he's left any, I think I might have missed dinner, and possibly lunch."

"Come on, let's get inside," Swift said, wrapping his arms around himself.

It had gotten colder. The warm April sun, replaced with a chill that seemed to be coming straight from the Antarctic.

"It's unlike Page to leave me on read for so long," Tink added, her usual casual tone replaced by something more urgent. "And I've called him a dozen times. Straight to voicemail."

Annie's stomach coiled. "Work phone?"

Tink nodded, "And personal."

"That cake must be really good," Annie joked, but Tink and Swift looked about as amused as Annie felt.

Annie hesitated in the doorway to the barn. It had been readjusted so it sat flush against the surrounds, but it didn't look as though it was secured to anything.

Swift clocked her hesitation. "Something wrong?"

She swallowed. "I don't know. Did Page say he was definitely meeting Clara here? This whole place looks out of bounds now. Like, how is this door even a door?"

A gust of wind moaned, a low, hollow sound against the building. Wrapping itself around Annie's ankles like cold fingers, her skin prickled. She took a slow breath and pulled at the handle.

For a split second, she saw something move in the reflection of the glass.

A shape. A shadow.

She whirled around, heart hammering in her chest, but there was nothing there except Swift and Tink, who were now looking at her like she had two heads.

"Did you see that?" Annie asked.

Tink was pale, her normally smiling face pinched with worry. But she shook her head in reply. Probably just hunger and tiredness, that's all. Still, Annie didn't turn her back to the glass in the doors as she pulled them open, their remaining hinge clinging on like a snake coiling around its prey.

She led the way to the cafe entrance, the overhead lights on and bright and welcoming. And, behind one of the tables by the window, Annie saw a figure slumped on the floor.

Her stomach dropped.

"Swift—"

He was already running towards it, pushing the chairs out of his way as he went.

"Call an ambulance," he shouted back.

Annie swiped her phone from her pocket and dialled 999, hurrying to the prone figure. A frenzy of panic buzzed in her mind, completely knocking her for six, Annie was certain that she was about to round the table and see Page lying there as dead as Eliza had been. As dead as Vivienne. She stopped at the figure's feet, tears clouding her vision.

Blinking them away, she saw that the person on the floor wasn't Page, but Clara. And she was still alive.

"Ambulance, please, quickly," Annie blurted at the call handler who answered. "My name is Annie O'Malley, I'm with Norfolk Police. I've got a young female, late twenties, collapsed. Badly beaten. She's unconscious but she's breathing, I think, hold on."

Annie lifted the phone from her face and raised her brows questioningly at Swift who was knelt beside Clara, blood seeping into his trousers. He nodded briskly back, fingers on Clara's pulse point on her neck, face tilted so he could see the rise and fall of her chest.

"Yes," Annie went back to the call. "Breathing but unresponsive. We're putting her in the recovery position. No, we're not in danger, whoever did this to Clara has long since…"

Annie's arm wobbled as she realised that they could be in danger. And even if they weren't, their friend could be.

"Tink," Annie shouted to the DS. "Try Page again."

Tink was already on her phone, but she shook her head.

"Call it in." Swift ordered Tink. "And tell them we might have an officer down."

Tink looked like she was about to keel over, but she drew an inner strength from somewhere and made the call to the station.

"Annie?" Swift was crouching beside Clara and Annie dropped to her knees to help him move her.

She put her phone on the floor so the emergency service handler could talk if she needed to and then gently lifted Clara's arm and tucked her fingers into her chin so they could roll her into the recovery position. The young woman curled in on herself, breathing shallowly. Blood stained her hair a bright pink that made Annie's pulse claw up her throat.

Clara let out a groan.

"Clara?" Swift said, softly. "Can you hear me? It's the police, you're safe. Can you tell me if you're hurt anywhere? Who did this to you?"

Annie wanted to desperately gouge more information from her. To ask about Page, the man who always put others first and who was a lifeline to his aging grandma. He would never harm anyone, and now it was looking like someone might have harmed him.

"Swift," Annie whispered. "There's so much blood."

She knew he was thinking the same thing. Head wounds were renowned for bleeding like a broken water geyser, but even so. The pool of it beside Clara looked too much for it to just be hers.

She groaned again, shifting slightly. Her eyes fluttered open, hazy with pain.

"Clara, what happened?" Annie asked.

Clara blinked slowly, dazed. "I—"

Her breathing hitched, like even speaking hurt. But her eyes flickered past them, toward the door, like she was afraid someone was still watching. Annie followed her gaze, but the rest of the cafe was empty, bar Tink who was still frantically calling Page.

Whoever had done this was long gone. Or… had never left at all. Annie shoved that thought aside, focusing back on Clara.

The young woman swallowed hard, wincing slightly. "I... I don't know."

Annie frowned. "You didn't see them?"

Clara hesitated. A fraction of a second. A breath too long.

Then she shook her head. "No. They must've hit me from behind."

"Stay with her," Swift said, as the tinny voice of the call handler advised the ambulance was two minutes away. "I'm going to look around."

"Swift," Annie hissed. "Is that wise? Shouldn't we wait for backup?"

"My man might be out there." Swift got up and put a hand on Annie's shoulder. "I'll be careful. See if Clara knows where Page is."

He disappeared into the stairwell and Annie turned back to Eliza's assistant as Tink came to sit beside them.

"Nothing." Tink offered an answer before Annie had even asked.

Her stomach sank.

"Clara, we're looking for someone," Annie said, taking Clara's hand. "DS Tom Page. The officer who was meeting you here. Do you know where he is?"

Clara's brows furrowed slightly, like she was trying to think through fog. "Who?"

Annie nodded. "Yes. DS Tom Page. You would have been talking about Eliza and the painting of Margot with him. We can't get hold of him and we need to know where he is and if he's safe."

Clara's expression didn't change. She blinked.

"I don't know who that is." Her voice was flat.

Annie felt the words land like ice water down her spine. She exchanged a glance with Tink, reading the exact same unease in his expression.

"Maybe he had an emergency with his gran," Annie whispered to Tink. But they both knew deep down that Page would have let them know where he was if that was the case. "Or maybe her head injury has given her short term memory loss?"

"Clara," Tink said slowly, carefully, like she was talking to a frightened animal. "The officer who was supposed to be here. Are you saying he never arrived?"

Clara shook her head and cried out with the movement, her face taking on the sheen of someone about to throw up. Annie needed her to keep her head as still as possible in case of neck injury, so she shuffled her own legs under her so she was sitting rather than crouching, and placed her hands gently either side of Clara's face.

"There was nobody else here." Clara said. "It was just me. I needed some of Eliza's paperwork. There's… something, I was doing something… I can't remember."

"Don't worry, Clara," Annie said, stroking the woman's hair with her thumbs. "It's because you've had a nasty bash to the head. I'm sure it will all come back to you soon."

"I don't want it to." Clara sniffed, a tear running

down the side of her temple and onto Annie's hand. "I don't want to go through it again. I'm scared."

"I know," Annie said, by way of comfort. "It'll be okay, you're safe now. We're here and we'll stay until the ambulance arrives."

"Are you sure you can't remember an officer coming to talk to you, Clara?" Tink pressed. "He's built like an ox; you should remember him. He's... he's."

Tink's bottom lip started to shake and Annie gave her a small smile.

It'll be okay she mouthed to Tink, comforting everyone as best she could as Swift strode back into the cafe.

Annie made a wish that Page would be right behind him, that it was all a big misunderstanding and Page's phone had died or he had no reception. But as Swift approached, his expression was dark.

"It's empty." He ran a hand through his hair. "No sign that anyone has been up there since the break-in."

"I wondered if Page might have had an emergency with his gran." Annie's hopes had been dashed already, surely not again.

"I just spoke to her care team," Swift replied. "She's fine. They're going to send an extra shift to help her, just until Page shows up."

Annie heard his voice catch. It was too much to bear.

"You think whoever came after Clara came face to face with Page?" Tink asked, quietly.

"And if they were here to tie up loose ends—" Annie whispered, indicating the woman lying in front of her.

The realisation hit like a punch to the gut. Because if someone *had* been tying up loose ends, then silencing a police officer would be high on their list.

SEVENTEEN

Swift drove like a man possessed. There was one place, and one place only they knew they had to get to. Brannon's. Everything was leading them to the shady art collector and Swift was doing his best to break the world land record to find him.

The wheels screeched as he took the corner, the car lurched forward with a surge of acceleration, the headlights cutting through the darkness in beams that bounced off the verges and little else. Annie's heart pounded, her fingers gripping the door handle as she tried to suppress the sinking feeling that was coiling in her gut.

Page was missing. Clara had been attacked.

"We should've dragged Brannon in the second we knew he bought that warehouse," Annie called out. "What if he's done something to Page?"

"Don't beat yourself up, Annie," Swift replied, his hands clenched around the wheel, knuckles stark white in the dim glow of the dashboard. "We were building a case. It's what we do. We didn't have enough concrete evidence to bring him in. We had suspicions."

"And now we have a missing officer. Friend. Page is the best human."

"And he'll continue to be the best human when we find him."

Annie checked her phone, keeping one hand as a weight on the car door to stop herself from flying around in the passenger seat. Tink had messaged. The DS had stayed behind with Clara when the ambulance had arrived. She was going to travel into the hospital behind them and keep an eye on the young woman. Really, Annie knew that Tink was waiting to pounce as soon as Clara's memory returned, but having an officer keeping guard wasn't a bad thing. Someone had tried to do away with Clara and they could come back to finish the job. There was also the small matter of *why* they'd tried to kill Eliza's assistant. What did she know that was worth her life?

Tink's message was brief. She was at the hospital. Clara was being patched up and checked over by the doctors and nurses. She still had no memory of the incident. Annie dropped Tink a quick reply as she relayed the messages to Swift.

"We can't rely on Clara," Swift said. Annie baulked at his words until she realised he meant her memory rather than her as a person. "We need to get to Brannon. He can fill in the gaps that Clara's assault has left."

Spurred on by his own words, Swift pressed the pedal harder, and they sped out onto the main road.

Brannon's estate loomed ahead, looking and feeling a whole lot different to the last time they were here. A dark silhouette against the night sky. The long, tree-lined drive stretched out like a tunnel, the gnarled branches arching overhead, their bare limbs clawing at the sky.

Swift didn't slow as they turned onto the gravel path, the tyres crunching over loose stones, the sound too loud in the oppressive silence of the night. Annie swallowed, staring ahead at the house as it came into view. In the daylight, it had looked imposing and elegant. Now, in the dead of night, with the headlights cutting stark white beams across the gravel drive and up the empty steps, it looked haunting, the darkness of the windows like clusters of spider's eyes against the creamy surrounds.

Swift rolled to a stop, letting the engine idle. Neither of them moved, as they watched the house. When he eventually killed the motor, the silence that pressed in felt thick. Even the trees—so dense and alive as they'd driven in—seemed to have gone still.

"Christ." Swift puffed out his cheeks.

Annie didn't need to ask what he was swearing about, she felt it too. Inside that house, there were answers that they desperately needed. But neither of them had taken the initiative to run to the door and demand them. It felt like the moment they stepped out of the car, something would step up beside them?

But they had come all this way. Page was in trouble. They had to move. Without another word, Swift pushed open his door, the creak of the hinges slicing through the quiet like a blade. Annie followed, stepping onto the gravel that crunched too loudly beneath her boots.

The house was even worse up close. The windows were black mirrors, swallowing the dim light from the moon and giving nothing back. Annie's gaze drifted to the doors as Swift headed to peer into the closest window, his hands cupped around his face against the glass.

She stood frozen, her skin prickling, feeling watched despite believing no one was out here with them. At least—no one they could see. There were acres of land around them, trees and brush and even the jutting brickwork of the house that would provide the perfect hiding spot for someone out to watch. She peered behind her, a cold tickle creeping up her neck and ruffling her hair like fingers of a stalker.

The wind shifted, rustling the trees. Annie turned back toward the door, lifting a hand to the brass bell. The sound echoed through the silence, swallowed instantly by the dark. She waited for a moment, but there was no response. Swift was still at the windows, peering in the next one, his shoulders tense around his ears.

"Something's not right."

Annie felt each second stretch, the silence pressing against her like something physical. The bell's echo had long since faded, leaving behind nothing but the pulse of her own heart in her ears.

"I'm trying the door," Swift said, jogging up the steps to join Annie.

He gripped the large round doorknob in his hands and twisted, pushing against the wood with his shoulder. But it didn't budge.

"Where is Brannon?" Annie whispered. "Where's his wife? His bloody butler?"

Swift stepped back and looked up at the floors above, his frown deepening.

"We need another way in," he said.

Annie nodded, glancing toward the side of the building. "There's got to be some sort of staff entrance around the back. Or patio doors somewhere. We might have more luck there."

Though she wasn't keen to head around the side of the house where the darkness looked heavier and the foliage thicker, Annie kept Page front and centre in her mind and figured she could deal with her fear of the dark in order to help him.

They moved slowly, boots crunching against the gravel, rounding the side of the sprawling mansion. The house stretched on and on, its walls rising high like a fortress. Every single window was muted in blacks. Nowhere was there the warmth of a fire crackling or a sconce spreading its light up the walls. Not even Brannon's picture lights were switched on, and

Annie couldn't imagine Brannon walking around his giant property switching off every individual light atop the paintings he hoarded.

The trees rustled behind them, shifting just enough to make Annie's stomach tighten. Every instinct told her to turn back, to look over her shoulder. But she didn't. She focused on the back of Swift's head in front of her, his broad shoulders silhouetted against the moonlight, and the thought that Page could be somewhere in this building, hurt and in need of their help.

A little thought snuck its way in. That someone else would get to them first. She shook her head and stepped a little quicker as they reached a narrow side door, set back into an alcove. Swift tried the handle but this one, too, was locked.

Swift exhaled through his nose.

"There's a terrace," he uttered, gesturing ahead. "Might have a way in up there."

Annie nodded, following as they crept further around the mansion.

The terrace stretched out before them, a wide, open space of smooth stone that must have looked beautiful during the day—overlooking the perfectly manicured gardens, bathed in sunlight, dotted with elegant outdoor furniture. Now, under the smothering darkness, it looked cold and exposed. A space meant for entertaining, now silent and empty.

A single set of French doors stood at the far end, their glass panes reflecting nothing back but the faint glow of the moon. Swift tested the handle. Locked. Of course. Annie glanced at him. A moment between them that said a thousand words as he pulled something small and thin from his pocket, crouching beside the handle. Annie watched, heartbeat thudding, as he worked quickly to wiggle the pick in the lock until a satisfying click sounded out. The door shifted slightly in its frame.

"Patio doors left unlocked," Annie whispered. "Not very safety conscious of a man with millions of pounds worth of art inside."

Swift's lips lifted in a small grin.

"Don't tell Robins."

"As if I would" Annie replied, smiling back, then she pushed open the doors.

The house swallowed them whole as they stepped inside, the air immediately cooler. Annie shivered, crossing her arms over her chest to keep her own warmth close.

The room they had entered was large, probably much like most of the rooms in the estate. A grand sitting room, lined with dark furniture, oil paintings hanging in ornate frames, a fireplace cold and untouched. Swift flicked on his torch, the beam cutting through the gloom, illuminating dust motes that floated like ghosts.

"Do we call out?" Annie asked. "Let them know we're police?"

"We should, yes," Swift said, edging further into the room. "But something feels really off about this.

It's like a show home, I feel like we're on the set of the Shein version of Downton Abbey and everyone has gone home for the night."

Annie snorted, despite the hideous situation they found themselves in, Swift was still able to make her laugh.

"Let's find our way to the front of the house and see how we feel then," Swift went on. "Stay close."

Annie didn't need to be told twice. They advanced deeper into the sitting room, past a heavy, glass-topped coffee table and an absurdly expensive-looking leather armchair. More grotesque sculptures like the ones Brannon had displayed in his office. The scent of polish and old fabric lingered in the air, but beneath it was something else. A faint, metallic tang. Annie's stomach tightened.

"Swift," she hissed. She knew that smell.

"I know," he said. "I can smell it too."

She put a hand on his shoulder, edging around so she could walk next to him rather than in his shadows. She stepped forward, just as her boot caught on something soft and malleable.

"Shit." She stumbled and Swift's torch beam jerked, sweeping down to her feet.

And there, sprawled out face down on the floor, was the body of a man in a pool of blood so large, Annie had thought it was an ornate carpet.

Page? Bile rose in her throat as she fell forwards, hands on her knees to stop her from landing next to the dead.

EIGHTEEN

DS Tom Page had been caught up with the wrong crowd back when he was at school. His dad hadn't cared enough to protect him from drugs and alcohol and all the men his mum would bring home. Page had battled demons by the age of thirteen that would knock most adults to their knees. And still he'd risen. Taken in by his gran, given the childhood he deserved and the ability to flourish in what he was good at. And what he was good at was people. Page was nuanced and calm. A great detective. And an even better person.

Had his battle been for nothing?

Annie's breath hitched, her vision tunnelling as she stared at the crumpled form on the floor. The blood spread wide and glistening, seeping into the intricate weave of the carpet like ink spilling from an overturned bottle.

Page. Her stomach lurched as she pictured the

uniformed officers heading to Page's home, hats off as a mark of respect. They'd sit down with his gran and tell her what had happened. Would she understand? Maybe it would be better for everyone if this was a truth that never sank in, instead it could sit on the surface of her dementia like oil on water.

Annie forced herself to move, to breathe, her fingers digging into her thighs as she leaned forward, pulse pounding in her skull.

"Page," she whispered, her voice barely there. "I'm so sorry. We should have protected you."

Swift was already crouching, reaching out, his torchlight catching the edge of the dead man's face. He drew back with a sharp intake of breath.

"Annie," he cried. "Annie, oh my god, it's not him. It's not Page."

The words didn't sink in right away. Annie blinked, her mind still stuck on the worst and bracing for the unbearable. Then, finally, she saw what Swift had seen. The greying hair and arms that were about half the size of Page's biceps hidden away in a stiff black uniform. The dead man wasn't DS Tom Page.

Annie let out a breath so sharp it hurt. Her hands trembled as she pressed them to her knees, grounding herself with the sharp bite of her own fingers.

"I think it's Brannon's butler," Swift confirmed grimly, pressing two fingers to the man's neck, though they both knew it was useless.

"Christ," Annie whispered, standing slowly, trying to force herself to think straight. "Thank god."

Then a stab of guilt gnawed at her stomach.

"I mean…" Annie started, pushing herself back upright and taking in the whole sorry mess.

"It's okay," Swift comforted. "I know what you meant. We're glad it's not Page. But that doesn't make us any less sad about the fact that a man has died here today. Probably a couple of hours ago, given the temperature and stiffness of the body."

"I'll call it in," Annie said, taking out her phone. "But I want to keep going, we need to find Page even more so now. There are too many dead people for him not to be in danger."

Swift shook his head, standing up and sweeping his torchlight around the room.

"We can't," he said. "It's too dangerous. This place is too big for us to search effectively. I should have realised that before we got here."

"Look at you being the sensible one in the duo for a change," Annie said, softly, as she dialled the station and relayed their situation. "There's a unit nearby, they'll secure the scene as soon as they get here. We need to meet them out the front of the building."

"Let's go." Swift gave the room one last look over and they exited the same way they'd come in.

Questions were whirring through Annie's head as Swift pushed the patio doors shut and took the stone steps down to where she was waiting.

"How were all the doors locked up if there's no one home except a dead man?" she asked as they walked back the way they came.

"Good question," Swift agreed. "Unless our killer is still inside? Or maybe there are doors we haven't found yet. Probably that. It's a huge place, there must be doors around the other side, maybe one of those is unlocked. I'll get uniform to do a thorough sweep."

The trees were lit up with the blues of the patrol car speeding down the driveway as they rounded the front of Brannon's estate. Swift went to meet the officers, unlocking the car so Annie could get inside and wait in the warmth. Her teeth chattered and she relished the heated seats as she leant over and pushed the ignition button. Her shoulders slumped, adrenaline seeping from her pores and rendering her liquified.

It wasn't Page. But that didn't mean Page was okay. If anything, it meant the opposite.

Someone had killed Brannon's butler and Page was still missing. Who would want to kill the butler? Butlers were the age-old answer to who did it, not normally the victims. Had Brannon killed him? Did the butler know too much? Maybe he'd stumbled across the abduction of a police officer and that was too much to keep quiet about.

Swift didn't speak as he climbed into the car, only the sound of his fingers drumming the wheel as he reversed sharply and peeled away down the long drive.

"Uniforms are going to sweep the house," he said, answering her unspoken question. "We'll hear as soon as they find anything. I told them about Page and they looked pretty pissed. If he's there, they'll find him."

Annie nodded, staring out at the darkness, her mind racing. They had a dead body, Page was still missing, and no sign of Brannon.

The worst part? That gnawing feeling she couldn't shake, like they were missing something huge—something lurking just beneath the surface, waiting for them to piece it together.

She tapped the dash. "Clara."

Swift frowned. "What?"

"She's the only one who can tell us what happened to Page."

Swift nodded, shifting gears, pushing the car faster. "Hospital's twenty minutes away," he said. "Let's hope that Tink has managed to jog Clara's memory."

Clara looked worse under fluorescent lighting. She was propped up in the hospital bed, her face pale, bruises deepening into purples and blues, a white bandage wrapped tight around her temple. Tink was sitting in the chair beside her, arms folded, watching her like a hawk. The DS glanced up when Swift and Annie walked in, bouncing out of her chair.

"Page?" She looked between the two of them with hope deep in the crease between her eyes.

Annie shook her head. "Nothing yet, you?"

"No." Tink sat back down with a thud. "She's talking, though. Sort of."

Clara shifted, looking between them. "Look, I'm sorry I can't remember what happened. I know you're feeling bad about your missing colleague, but I am too."

Annie's skin prickled. She wanted to tip Clara upside down and shake the memories out of her.

"We'll find him," she said instead, trying to persuade herself as much as anyone else. "Do you remember anything? Can you remember why you were up at the studio for a start?"

Clara frowned, the bandage pushing her brows down over her eyes. She blinked a few times to unstick her lashes from her forehead.

"I… I'm not sure, I think I was looking for something," Clara replied, slowly, eyes cast upwards. "Or… no, that's not it. I wanted to take the painting."

Her cheeks coloured and she looked down at the thin NHS blanket.

"The unfinished portrait?" Annie asked.

They stood either side of the head of Clara's bed, machines beeping and whirring in the ward around them, but Clara's bedside was thankfully free of IV drip stands and monitors.

"I… maybe," Clara whispered. "Actually, yeah, you're right. I think I was there to meet your colleague."

"Our officers weren't able to find your phone at the scene," Swift added. "Did you have it on you when you arrived?" He turned to Tink. "Do you have Clara's bag of personal belongings?"

"In the bedside cupboard," Tink replied. "But I don't remember seeing a phone."

The flush on Clara's cheeks vanished. "That phone is my life. I need it." She looked like she was about to cry.

"I'll ask the officer to look again," nodded Swift. "I just wanted to see if you had any calls from Page, or messages with his arrangements on them. Tink, can you check to see where we're at with tracing Page's phone."

"On it." Tink pushed up from her chair and scampered out of the room, as though she'd been waiting for an opportunity to leave.

Annie turned back to Clara who was chewing on the inside of her cheek, her hands twisted upon her blanket.

"What do you think made you say you were looking for the painting?" she asked, curious.

"I don't know," Clara confessed. "Stupid really, seeing as it's been lost."

"Yeah," Annie agreed. "Not stupid, your brain is probably playing tricks on you. I'm sure you didn't go looking for it. I'm just intrigued as it was the first thing that sprang to mind. You could have been there to see any of the works of art, but you said the unfinished portrait. Clara, we need you to tell us what Eliza was hiding in the painting. Why was she so afraid of it?"

Clara blinked slowly, her movements deliberate, like she was weighing every word before she spoke.

"That painting is a curse," she murmured, eyes glazing over.

A chill skittered down Annie's spine. Swift folded his arms over his chest, but just before he did so, Annie saw him shiver too. Clara's gaze flicked up to the DI, and for the first time since they'd arrived, Annie saw real fear there.

"It's dangerous," she whispered. She leaned forward, her voice barely audible. "You're in danger."

The words hung in the air, thick and suffocating. Annie exchanged a look with Swift, unease coiling in her gut. Clara exhaled, her fingers tugging at the hospital blanket, twisting the fabric between them tighter, until the folds of her wrists were red raw.

"Eliza tried to fix it," she said. "She thought if she painted over it, she could—" She let out a sharp, bitter breath. "But it's not something you can just hide."

"Hide what? What do you mean, Clara?" Annie pressed.

"Anyone who has seen it is at risk."

Annie's stomach dropped. Her mind flashed to the painting, to Margot's bruised face, half-buried under layers of paint. To Vivienne, dead in her gallery. To Eliza, lifeless on her studio floor. To Page, missing. The feeling that something had been watching her. She hadn't believed it before, putting the eerie feelings down to being tired or stressed or in the wrong place at the wrong time.

Clara's voice was quiet, barely above a breath. "Margot won't stop until the truth is out."

The words sent a ripple of ice through Annie's veins. She could tell by the way Swift's jaw tightened that he felt it too.

"Clara, what do you mean?" Swift asked, but the young woman had shut her eyes and her chin lolled against her chest. "What do you know about Margot?"

"I'm tired," she whispered. "Let me be."

Annie waved across the bed to Swift, catching his attention. She gave him a quick nod and they huddled by the drawn curtain around Clara's bed.

"It's late," she said. "We're exhausted and stressed. Why don't we head back to your's to recoup for a couple of hours? There are officers out looking for Page, we're waiting to trace his phone. Brannon is on the run somewhere, but we have no idea where to start looking. We're no use to anyone like this."

"Okay," Swift agreed, pulling the curtain back and letting Annie go first. "Just a couple of hours."

Annie stirred the hot chocolate, the spoon clinking against the ceramic mug, her grip a little too tight. Her body ached for rest, but her mind was still wired, buzzing and unwilling to switch off.

Swift had gone to shower, leaving her alone in the kitchen, the warm glow from the under-cabinet lights casting soft pools across the counters. Outside, beyond the large windows, the garden stretched out into nothingness. Annie didn't want to look, but she couldn't help but be drawn to the darkness. The glass reflected the room back at her, her own face pale, but beyond that the garden seemed to swallow the light.

Annie swallowed, suddenly aware of how alone she was down here. She turned back to the hot chocolate, shaking her head.

Get a grip.

But then. A movement, so small she almost missed it. Her pulse lurched and she snapped her gaze back to the garden. There was nothing there. Just the hedges. The trees. The dark expanse of lawn. Her fingers tightened around the counter. It had been nothing. A trick of the light. A shift in her own reflection.

Then it happened again. A flicker. A ripple of shadow shifting where nothing should be moving. Her breath hitched. She stepped back from the counter, her skin crawling and she forced herself to take a deep breath, but it did nothing to calm the unease gripping her chest. She turned back to her cup, willing herself to just focus.

A tap.

Barely a sound. Just the lightest pressure against the glass. Annie froze. She didn't look to see who was knocking on the glass. Clara's warnings ripe in her mind. *You're in danger.* She counted to three in her head, willed her legs to move. She left the half-made hot chocolate on the counter and moved, fast and silent, up the stairs to the safety of Swift.

NINETEEN

WEDNESDAY

ANNIE WOKE WITH A START, SHOCKED TO SEE THE SUN streaming through the gaps in the curtains. She hurried out of bed and washed and dressed with the speed of an Olympic athlete. There was no sign of Swift, but she guessed he was down in the kitchen as the smell of frying bacon wafted up the staircase and made her stomach churn with hunger. Hurrying down, Annie grabbed her phone from the bedside table and saw she had a missed call from Tink.

Page. She ran faster.

"Tink rang," Annie called out, rounding the bottom of the grand staircase and running to the kitchen, cursing the size of Swift's house. "I can't believe I slept for so long."

Swift was at the hob, dressed in his usual crisp shirt and dark trousers, turning bacon with calm efficiency. The toaster popped, making Annie jump away from the inanimate object.

"Sit," Swift commanded as he poured her a coffee and buttered the slices of toast. "It's only six, you didn't sleep for long at all."

He added an obscene amount of bacon to each slice and a good dollop of ketchup for Annie, then came to join her at the island.

"Tink called," she repeated, reaching over for her plate with a thanks. "Have you spoken to her?"

"Not yet." Swift put his phone on the marble countertop and dialled Tink, his fingers leaving greasy marks on his screen.

Tink picked up on the second ring and Swift hit speaker.

"Any news about Page?" Swift was straight in with the important question.

"Nothing yet," Tink replied. "It's driving me crazy, guys. I couldn't sleep. I just kept thinking he must be so scared and wondering when the bloody hell we're going to turn up to rescue him. At least, that's if he's still a—"

"Tink," Annie interrupted, not wanting to hear what Tink was about to say. "Stay positive. Officers were going over Brannon's place last night, and they'll be able to see more now the sun is up. Have we managed to trace his phone yet?"

"It's switched off," Tink's voice wobbled. "We can't trace it if it's switched off."

Swift tapped at the marble with his knuckles, his breakfast sitting untouched.

"We need to break this down, we're missing

something, I can feel it." Annie took a bite of her bacon sandwich and felt the warmth feeding her whole body.

"Annie's right." Swift said. "This case started with a dead artist and an unfinished painting linked to a missing woman. What haven't we managed to work out yet? Something glaringly obvious, as every time we've been anywhere near that portrait you guys have felt uneasy."

"The real connection between Eliza and Margot," Tink cried.

Annie would have said it herself had it not been for her mouthful. They'd been so fixated on the separate parts of this case that the two women at the centre of it had stayed in their own bubbles, a brief crossover like a Venn with no correlation, when really their intersection should read more like a logical relationship.

"We know they knew each other," Annie added. "That they hung out back before Margot went missing."

"We also know that Eliza painted Margot covered in bruises." Tink's voice cut out briefly. "Sorry, am out for a run and I just went through the underpass."

"Christ," Swift huffed. "Look after yourself. Clara said that anyone who's seen the painting is in danger."

"Yeah," Tink called back. "She said that to me too. I think she was talking about its ghostly presence rather than anything physically dangerous."

"You don't believe it's got… I don't know, something going on with it?" Annie leant over the phone.

"Nope," Tink replied. "I don't believe in ghosts. Though…"

"What?" Swift pressed.

"Nah, nothing, it's nothing. Probably just tired and stressed and that, my dear friends, is why I'm out for a run. You should try it."

Swift raised a brow at Annie who agreed entirely with his sentiments.

"Oh, what, hold on." The sound of Tink's footsteps stopped.

"Everything okay?" Annie asked, panic bubbling in her already cauldroning chest. "Tink?"

Tink's breathing didn't sound like she'd been out for a run. It was calmer than Annie's.

"Yeah, sorry," she replied. "I'll have to call you back, the auctioneer from where I picked up the portrait is calling me."

"Noah Centineo?" Annie grinned.

"That's the one, well Ben Harebell, but yes," Tink replied. "Speak soon."

She hung up and Annie looked at Swift who was eyeing her curiously.

"Good memory, O'Malley," he said, warily.

"Jealous, Swift?" Annie replied, taking another bite of sandwich.

"Er, yes," he said, surprisingly honest. "Bet he wouldn't make you breakfast fit for a queen as often as I do."

Annie chewed thoughtfully. Swift was more than his bacon sarnies, he was kind and compassionate and caring and funny and hot. She blew him a kiss.

"Tink would poke my eyes out with the nearest sharp object if I even thought about it." She winked at him as he narrowed his eyes. "Now, while Tink is flirting something chronic with a young auctioneer, we need to be looking into the connection between Eliza and Margot."

"Agreed." Swift vanished out the kitchen and Annie took the time to clear up their dishes and finish her coffee.

She was wiping the surfaces when he returned with his laptop and a stack of paperwork.

"So, where do we start?" He set his computer down on the island and flipped open the lid.

"Old case files?" Annie said, sitting back down. "We need to find out if Eliza was interviewed about the disappearance of Margot. It'd be a massive red flag if she wasn't."

"It was a gross oversight that Brannon's name didn't even flag up when he bought the warehouse." Swift was typing as he talked. "So I wouldn't hold your breath. While you're doing that, I'm going to make some calls about Page. It's been over twelve hours since we last knew of his whereabouts and I am worried about him."

Annie stroked Swift's arm.

"We all are," she said. "I am finding it really hard to sit here and read case files when I want to get out there and look for him. It's like my legs won't stay still. I feel antsy. My brain is struggling to think of anything other than the need to get on the road and get looking for Page. But I also know that our best bet is to work out what it is we're not seeing in Eliza's case. Because there are officers out there looking for Page who have way better resources for this kind of thing than we do."

"Breathe, Annie," Swift said, placing a hand over hers. "I know exactly what you mean and I also know that this will make us better detectives in the long run. Give us an insight into what the families of the missing are going through. I think a little empathy… oh, crap, sorry Annie."

She was looking at him with a face that spoke a thousand words, most of them about how she knew exactly what those families were going through already. Not being a stranger to missing people; Annie's sister and dad had been missing for years before she managed to track them down, mostly argue with them, and then lose them to the world again. She knew.

"It's okay," she said. And it really was okay. Her past wasn't her present. And her present was all she needed. "You go and talk to the squad; I'll get on with this. Let me know as soon as you hear anything."

Swift kissed the top of her head and headed out the kitchen into the hall. Moments later, Annie heard the door to the garden clicking shut and she directed her attention to the original case files scattered on the island. Pulling the stack toward her, the pages yellowed at the edges, she took a deep breath, rolling her shoulders before diving in.

Margot Grayson. Missing person.

Her file was thin, not overly packed with reports or interviews, though there was an old, grainy photograph of a smiling young woman who had vanished into nothing. Eliza's name appeared just a couple of times. Not as a suspect, not even as someone of interest, but as a footnote. Someone who had been spoken to briefly, her statement barely more than a single paragraph buried in pages of speculation.

Eliza Warren, local artist, states she knew Margot through social circles. Last saw her at an exhibition the night before her disappearance. Claims no knowledge of personal relationships or whereabouts on the night of incident.

Annie frowned, flipping the page. That was it? A missing woman. A known connection between them. A portrait, unfinished. And Eliza had barely been spoken to? She flipped further, scanning the handwritten notes from the original detectives—old-school scribbles, shorthand, barely legible.

> *Spoken to at her residence. Appeared distracted. Provided a brief statement but declined to answer further questions at the time. Subject seemed concerned about being overheard. Appeared protective of the child. Interview kept brief.*

Annie started. A child. They knew that Eliza had no family to pass down items to following her death, what had happened to the child? She rifled through the next few pages. There was no follow-up. No additional notes. No record of anyone ever checking Eliza's statement again. No wonder Dominic Grayson had been so angry about the investigation into his sister's disappearance, they'd really let him down. They'd let Margot down.

She put down the files and hitched off the stool just as Swift marched back into the kitchen.

"I was just coming to find you," she said, ready to tell him about the child in the statement.

"The officers have already left Brannon's," he blurted.

"What?"

"Apparently they did a once over and left after Evans' team arrived."

"But that's not long enough to look everywhere, his home is huge."

"I know," Swift growled. "I've told them my feelings."

Annie was about to suggest they head back to the estate when his phone rang out through the kitchen.

"Tell me you've got something, Tink," he barked, skipping pleasantries.

"I've got something," Tink replied, urgently. "I called the auctioneer back."

Annie straightened. "And?"

"He put a shout out for dash cam footage for the night when the portrait was dropped off, on the off chance any of his regulars were parked up, or any of the farm workers were about. He got a positive."

With their full attention zeroing in on the call, the kitchen was so silent, Anne could hear her blood pumping through her veins.

"Who was it?" Annie asked, her pulse thudding.

"He's sending over the footage, but he said he thinks it looks like a young person."

"Male or female?" Swift asked.

"Probably female, though they had their hood up over a cap and their face was partially covered in shadow."

Annie's stomach dropped.

"A young woman?" she said, quietly.

Swift went rigid beside her, their eyes catching. There was only one person who was involved in this case who they both knew of. And that person had been lying to them.

Clara.

The name landed in her mind like a puzzle piece snapping into place. Clara had left the painting, which probably meant that Clara had taken the painting from the studio, causing all the damage as she had done so.

"Clara knew the painting was missing. She said so last night, why didn't I realise it then? There's no way she'd know that." Annie was frantic and Swift was already on the move. "We need to get back to the hospital Tink, we're on our way there now, meet you with Clara."

"On it. See you there."

Tink ended the call and Annie ran to the door behind Swift. Because if Clara had been lying to them all along, Page's life might depend on how fast they got back to her.

TWENTY

Swift dumped the car in an already overflowing car park and they ran, pushing through the automatic doors when they didn't open fast enough. Disinfectant and the clawing stench of breakfast hit Annie as she powered through the lobby close on Swift's heels.

They bypassed reception and the slow-moving lifts and ran up the stairs to the second floor. Annie's legs were burning and her lungs felt like they were full of water, but she kept going, finding Page front and centre of her mind. The corridor stretched out ahead of them, food trolleys and tabard clad workers blocked their paths, but they made it to the ward where Clara was admitted in record speed.

"Working for Eliza," Annie puffed, as they flashed their badges to the nurse on the ward desk through the window of the locked door, "Clara would have had a front row seat to all of her business. Why take the painting and try to secretly get rid of it? If she wanted it gone, why not destroy it, or why not take it to somewhere a little further away than Essex? It doesn't make sense."

"Maybe she couldn't bring herself to destroy it," Swift replied. "Maybe Essex felt far enough away."

Annie processed what Swift had said, a bubble of ideas forming in her mind.

"Do you think she was protecting Eliza's work or Margot's memory?"

"You can ask her when we see her."

The nurse swiped her badge and pulled open the door, letting Swift and Annie through into the ward with a smiley greeting. Despite the early hour, it was already full of hustle and bustle. A place that never slept. With minimal windows and the dull overheads, it could have been any time of day once they walked through the doors.

They marched straight to the bay where they'd talked to Clara only hours earlier. Her curtain was still drawn, hopefully they wouldn't have to wake her to talk to her, but if that's what was needed then Annie had no doubt that Swift wouldn't even falter. Annie grabbed the edge and tugged it back, revealing the uncovered window and Clara's bed, which was sitting empty. Annie glanced over her shoulder hoping to catch a glimpse of the woman somewhere on the ward or in the bay.

"Maybe she's getting washed, on the loo?" she

said, but Swift was already half running back to the ward station.

"Where is Clara Cresswell?" he asked the nurse who had sat herself back down with a mountain of paper notes.

"I'm sorry?" Her face flushed a little as she looked up at Swift. He always had that effect, even when he wasn't the politest.

"Clara Cresswell, she was in the bed by the window."

"Let me check for you," the nurse rolled her chair over to the computer tucked away behind another load of patient files on the desk; she clicked the mouse a few times.

"Thank you," Annie added, giving Swift a stern look. He had the decency to cringe and mouth *sorry* at her.

"Yep, here we go," the nurse said, peering closely at the screen. "Miss Cresswell discharged herself against hospital advice at around two this morning."

"What?" Annie and Swift said in unison.

"But she had a head wound," Annie gasped. "A bad one at that, surely she should have been made to stay."

The nurse wheeled her chair back to the detectives, shaking her head.

"No, we can't force people to stay if we believe they have capacity. It's all about informed choices, isn't it?"

"What about an informed choice not to put herself

at risk of dropping dead from a TBI or a blood clot?" Annie replied.

"From what I could see on her notes, the head wound wasn't all that bad. They just bleed a lot so they always look worse. Doctor patched her up and said to stay in for 24 hours in case she had a concussion, but the cut was long and not deep and wasn't really worthy of concussion once they'd cleaned it out. I honestly wouldn't worry about her dropping dead from a Traumatic Brain Injury any time soon."

"Cut?" Swift asked. "I thought it was a blow to the head?"

"Oh no," the nurse replied. "It looked more like a scrape or a slash if anything. Like a sharp, thin blade had sliced from back to front. But it looked pretty neat, and thankfully, missed the main branches of the occipital and the superficial temporal arteries."

Annie could see the surprise register on Swift's face. A carefully sliced cut from back to front wasn't the outcome of someone being whacked around the back of the head. And if Clara hadn't been hit with a blunt object, then it's likely she wasn't suffering from memory loss.

"So it's unlikely that Clara wouldn't be able to remember what happened to her, or what caused her injury?" Annie asked.

"Oh no," the nurse went on. "There was nothing to suggest memory loss or TBI or anything along those lines. In fact, her notes were quite minimal, mostly test results and a prescription for pain meds, and an opportunity to make an appointment to get her stitches taken out."

"Argh," Swift bashed his hands against the desk and made the nurse jump. "Sorry, sorry. That was out of order. I'm frustrated at myself, not you guys. You're the good guys here." He turned to Annie. "So she was lying about not knowing who did this to her. Maybe lying about not having seen Page. Where would she have gone?"

"The only address we have for Clara is Eliza's studio." Tink was running towards them with her phone pressed to her ear. "There's nothing else on file? Right, thanks, talk soon."

The three of them hurried back to Clara's bedside, mostly to get out of the way of the breakfast trolleys arriving on the ward. Swift pulled the curtain shut, gathering his team into the false sense of privacy it offered.

"Did we not take any other addresses for her?" he asked Tink.

"No," she replied, sitting on the edge of the bed. "That's all the first officer on the scene got. And I didn't think to ask as I don't normally take all the initial info, sorry guv."

"No, it's not your fault. It's not the fault of the first officer, either. Why would Clara give us that address and not her home address?"

Annie bent down to peer in the bedside cabinet on the off chance that Clara left behind some of her personal items that had been stashed in there earlier. But it was empty.

'She wasn't sleeping there, was she?" Swift asked, offering Annie an arm as she straightened back up. "There was no sign of anyone sleeping in the studio, from what I can remember."

"The old barn is pretty big though," Tink added.

But Swift was shaking his head, his lips pursed, not quite believing it. And Annie didn't either.

"No, I don't think she was sleeping at the barn," he said. "I have a feeling she just downright lied to us."

"Do you think she was scared?" Tink asked. "Hunted down by the same person who killed Eliza and Vivienne."

"I don't think she was being hunted by anyone," Annie replied, softly. "I think our Clara *is* the hunter."

Tink baulked.

"You think Clara knows more than she's letting on?" she asked. "If you don't think she's scared, then why didn't she tell us who attacked her?"

Annie sat down next to Tink like a sack of very tired potatoes. The bed creaked under her, the thin mattress tilting as though trying to tip her onto the floor.

"I mean exactly that," Annie went on. "Clara is the hunter. I think she sliced her own head open."

"What?" Swift's nose scrunched.

"You heard what the nurse said. Her scalp was cut from back to front. That says two things to me. Either someone was standing in front of Clara and leant around to slice her head open without so much as a *no thank you* from Clara. She had no defence wounds, which she would have if she was tackling a knife wielding psycho. Or—"

"She did it to herself." Tink blew out a breath as she spoke the same words as Swift.

"But why?" Swift asked.

"To throw us off the scent." Annie threw her hands in the air to emphasise her point. They were sitting on an empty hospital bed looking for a woman who was long gone. "Because she knew we were on to her."

"Page called her?" Tink offered. "Told her we were on our way to possibly collect the missing painting because he knew she'd be concerned about it. Probably wanted to say something kind before he told her we needed to talk to her again. Maybe he rattled her? She did something to him then hurried back to the studio and sliced open her head to make it look like she was the victim?"

"You looked around the studio, right?" Annie turned to Swift. "There was no sign of Page, was there?"

"No," Swift replied. "None at all and Robins had a fit and told me that three incidents in the one place warranted around-the-clock presence and my job might be on the line, so our officers would have found him by now."

Annie did a double take, unaware that Swift had

even talked to Robins, let alone been in trouble with their DCI.

"So, they must have met somewhere else. There's no way Clara could have overpowered Page and if she did, there's no way she could have moved him on her own," Annie said, brain whirring with scenarios.

"Unless she had help," Tink added.

A small cough from outside the curtain made them all spin around. Swift pulled it back to reveal the slight frame of the nurse who had been helping them.

"Sorry, I couldn't help but overhear your conversation," she said, nodding sheepishly to the thin material separating them from the next bay. "You're having trouble locating the woman who was in this bed?"

They all nodded.

"And am I right in thinking she might be in danger?" The nurse widened her eyes and dropped her chin, suggesting that they need to agree with her for her to disclose whatever information it was she had.

"Utmost danger," Annie said.

"Like, the worst danger you can imagine," Tink added, before whispering under her breath. "Well, she will be when I get my hands on her."

"Okay, well if you'd like to follow me back to the nurses station, I can look up her address on our system, seeing as you don't have it."

"She gave you her address?" Swift asked, walking alongside the nurse as Annie and Tink followed behind.

"Oh, no, she wasn't very forthcoming with us, either," she replied. "My colleague in A&E found it in her personal items, on her driving licence. She was supposedly unconscious when she got here. We will often look for next of kin details amongst personal items, especially if the patient is deemed at high risk of long-term injury or death."

She gave the team a conspiratorial smile, ducked around the desk, and logged back into the computer.

"We get this address, we get all units we can out there," Swift said, quietly to Annie and Tink.

"And we go straight there too, yeah?" Tink asked, though there was no way she was taking no for an answer.

Swift nodded. Somewhere in the ward an alarm beeped and a couple of nurses ran past the backs of the team, wafting with them a movement of stale air.

"Here we go," the nurse said, smiling. "Got a pen?"

Annie grabbed one from the desk and pulled a sticky note from the stack beside it.

"Go for it."

But when the nurse started to read out the address, Annie knew she didn't need the pen or the sticky note. Because Clara's address was Brannon's address too.

TWENTY-ONE

Annie didn't like this. Not one bit.

With the sun burning red through the new buds blossoming on the trees, it looked like hell. And felt like it. The car was silent and the cold was seeping in through the tinted windows. Annie rubbed her hands together and then tucked them into her pockets.

"Are we going in?" she said.

"No." Swift shook his head. "We need to wait for backup this time."

"Since when do you ever wait for backup?"

"Since a member of my team went missing," Swift replied.

Annie knew that wasn't true. She checked her watch and saw that it had only been two minutes since she last looked, which meant way too long before the cavalry would be arriving. Her fingers twitched near the door handle and Swift hit the lock.

"Really?" Annie raised a brow at him.

"Robins told me under no circumstances was I to let anyone into the house before the backup arrived," Swift snapped. "Sorry. I wish I could ignore her, but I have a feeling I'm on my last warning."

"But it's Page, and we're doing nothing for him sitting here." Annie slumped into her chair. "Why is Robins being so weird? Why can't she just let you be you, we always come out okay in the end?"

"I know, right?" Swift said, his own hand now resting near the door handle.

He was going to add something but there was a flash of yellow as Tink's car flew into the driveway and screeched to a halt next to them. It took the DS less than five seconds to kill the engine and burst from the driver's seat. And she was gone. Running towards the front door of Brannon's large family home without even a glance back to Swift's car and its occupants.

Swift pulled at the handle of his door, seemingly forgetting he'd just locked them in. Fumbling with the buttons he threw open the door and stuck his head out.

"Tink, stop, we have to wait, it's not safe."

Tink looked back over her shoulder as she ran. She gave Swift a look that could be boiled down to a hundred swear words all at once and carried on towards the front door.

"TINK." Swift shouted again.

Annie took her chance and pushed open her own

door, jumping down to the gravel and heading after Tink.

"Oh my god, Annie, Tink," Swift called, but Annie could hear the resolve seeping out of him. "Right, come on then, let's do this." He was at Annie's side in seconds.

Tink reached the door first, ducking under the blue tape, the double-sided entrance a great big wall of wood in front of her. She grabbed the handle and pushed and, much to Annie's surprise as she ran up the stone steps, the door swung open.

"The search team must have broken the lock." Swift said, taking the lead. "You guys need to stay right behind me. I'm not having you two come to harm or Robins won't just fire me, she'll erase me from the face of the earth."

"I think you're overestimating how much she likes us," Tink muttered.

"She likes me," Annie whispered back.

Tink flipped Annie the bird and blew her a kiss and then disappeared into the house. Annie could see the mist rising from her breath as she stepped across the threshold. It was about five degrees colder inside than it was out. Like all old homes, it sucked the dampness in from the air around it, holding it in its bones like a sponge, ready to squeeze over anyone who dared enter.

"I don't even know where to start." Swift had stopped in the giant entrance hallway, redundantly flicking a light switch.

The electricity must still be out, and even though it was a bright morning outside, the windows seemed to sieve the joy from the sunbeams as they passed through the glass.

"Shall we split up and check all the ground floor rooms?" Tink asked.

Swift's mouth twisted as he contemplated Tink's suggestion. It was foolish, but it might be the only way they got through the maze of doors ahead of them.

"No, but we move briskly and quietly. Come on."

They worked methodically, sweeping around the hallway starting with the first door on the left. Each room held no clues to Page's whereabouts, just a nod to Brannon's love of art and the size of his wealth. Through the inner hallway was his office, where Annie and Swift had been standing not so many days before. Empty. The kitchen was vast and soulless, not even the old scent of coffee or yesterday's cooked food lingered in the air. Empty.

"Where are they?" Swift hissed as they reached the back of the house and the room they'd broken into the night before. Blue tape crossed the door and Annie put a hand on Swift's as he went to pull it down.

"They're not here," she said. "Can't you feel it? This place is dead. Even the animals are taxidermised."

She threw her arm out to indicate a stuffed fox on

a plinth that stared at them with glassy eyes and a snarl.

"But Brannon lives here. With his wife, by all accounts. And Clara too?" Tink blew out a thin stream of air through pursed lips. "Do they all live in this mausoleum?"

"Let's go upstairs," Swift said. "I can hear the sirens, the back-up must be nearly here. We can sweep it over before we leave. No wonder it didn't take uniform long to clear out last night."

It felt like the last strands of hope were tugging loose from Annie's mind. And from the way that Tink and Swift trudged up the stairs, she figured they were feeling the same. Each marble step a stark reminder that no matter how large the home, if it wasn't lived in and wasn't loved then it could hide very few secrets.

The landing proved as stark as the ground floor had, though about half the size. A couple of marble plinths holding plaster heads and other forms of sculptures. They were chaotic, unfinished looking, and quite grotesque up close. A twisted mouth and a startled stare. Annie shook out her arms and caught up with the others.

"It feels a bit like a reverse Tardis up here," Tink said, opening a door and promptly closing it again. "Airing cupboard."

Tink was right. With only five doors to check, the first floor felt markedly smaller than its lower counterpart. Whereas the ground floor was deep as well as wide, this floor was only one room in depth.

"Hold on," Annie said, stepping back up to the door. "Why do none of these rooms look lived in?"

She opened the door and peered inside. The bed was neatly made but it was the empty bedside table and the lack of curtains that made alarm bells ring in Annie's ears. "I feel like this is a show home."

"I think it *is* a show home," Swift said, his voice muffled from outside the room. "Look."

Annie and Tink shut the door behind them and went to see what Swift was pointing to along the back wall of the landing.

"This wall is hollow," he said, tapping quietly on it. "In a house like this, walls should be brick and solid. I think there's something behind it. Spread out, look in the bedrooms either side and see if there's anything amiss. I think, whatever we're looking for is waiting for us behind this wall."

The women split up, Annie going back to the empty bedroom they'd just come from, Tink in the opposite direction. Swift took the landing, searching for an opening in the false wall.

Annie stood back and surveyed the space. There was a layer of dust covering the furniture, very unlikely if the room was regularly used. She exhaled slowly, feeling the tiny goose pimples scattering across her skin. It wasn't right. In fact, the whole house felt wrong, a carefully curated illusion, like a dollhouse with locked compartments.

She ran her hands along the edges of an ornate dresser, checking for anything out of place. Nothing. She turned to the wardrobe, pulling the doors open with a creak, maybe hoping to find a Narnia on the other side, Page waiting for her by a snowy lamppost. Empty. Annie's stomach twisted.

She moved toward the window, her reflection faintly visible in the glass. The edges of the garden stretched beyond, bathed in the dim, eerie light of the early morning. Something prickled at the back of her neck. A presence making themselves known. Annie froze.

Don't turn around.

Her breath hitched. The hairs on her arms rose. It was just a feeling. A trick of her overworked brain, exhaustion creeping in. She forced herself to move, to break the spell. It felt much like the same spell the unfinished portrait had over her when she'd seen it in Eliza's studio all the way back at the beginning of the case.

Just one step. Then another. The air shifted, as though something had moved with her. Annie spun instinctively, her heart slamming against her ribs. But there was nothing there. Just the empty room, the perfectly made bed.

She exhaled sharply, running a hand through her hair and pulling it up off her face in a messy ponytail with the band that had been cutting off the circulation to her hand.

Get a grip, O'Malley.

Then she saw it. A little door, hidden in plain sight to the side of the wardrobe. It sat flush to the wall, like an old, built in cupboard. Bare wooden slats looked quaint against the white-washed walls. She took a step closer, tilting her head, listening to the sounds coming from behind the door. The tinny laughter from a television show filtered through. Studio audience applause.

Annie froze. She felt sick to her stomach. This wasn't a cupboard door, there was a whole other room behind it.

"Swift, Tink," she whispered, running back to the landing. "It's here. Quick."

They ran back through, and Annie pointed out the door. "We didn't see it for looking."

"And the officers who swept the place last night probably thought it was a shelved cupboard, that's what these normally are." Swift pressed his ear to the door, holding a finger up to his lips. "Someone is in there."

"What do we do?" Tink asked.

"We wait," Swift whispered. "Back-up are downstairs. Let's send them up here and they can break down the door and play the hero this time."

Someone cried out from behind the door. The bloodcurdling scream of a grown man that made Annie's skin shrink on her bones.

"We don't wait," Tink cried, and she flicked the latch and pulled the door open.

TWENTY-TWO

The door swung open with a whisper of wood on wood, revealing not just a cupboard. Not even just a room made from hidden storage space. But a corridor. They stepped through into what felt like a normal entrance hallway of a family home. There was a coat hook piled with wax jackets, macs, scarves, and bags. Underneath was a pile of discarded shoes; a couple of pairs of brogues, trainers, and slip on shoes whose soles had seen better days.

The sounds of the television were louder now, the canned laughter made Annie think of post-school dinners in front of the telly, yet it was still early morning. Swift held a finger to his lips again but the last thing Annie felt like doing was making a noise. The atmosphere behind the door was so intense she could feel it pressing against her chest, rendering her diaphragm obsolete. She clawed in a breath through an open mouth and tried to ignore the stars gathering in the corners of her vision.

The walls were narrow, purpose built from slats of plasterboard with slapdash paint and a few cheap looking paintings and standard doors. Compared with the house it was buried in, this *home* for want of a better word, felt more like real life and less like the museum of its surroundings. Only the ceiling held the original grandeur, sky high and carrying the ornate plasterwork mouldings on its shoulders.

The scent of old air, of stale fabric and something else—something metallic—clawed at the back of Annie's throat. She looked to Tink whose face was puce, and Swift, who looked his usual focussed self. He motioned for them to follow behind him as he crept up the corridor to the first closed room.

The laughter from the tinny TV grew louder as they moved forward. The rhythmic applause of a studio audience rattled through the corridor, the occasional burst of static making the hairs on Annie's arms prickle.

Swift counted down with his fingers.

Three.

Two.

One.

Then he turned the handle and pushed open the door. With no windows and no lamps, the room flickered with the white light from the television as it cast a sickly glow over ugly brown furniture and a floral-patterned rug that had seen better days. The television was on the far wall, a sofa between the door and the TV. The backs of two heads were visible. One female, her greying hair like that of a mannequin, thinning and sticking out in all directions. One male, his shoulders hunched as he sat on the sofa, the television flickering in front of him. The sound of a game show host's voice blared out, deafeningly, from the speakers.

"Come on now, you know the answer!" The studio audience laughed.

Annie's stomach clenched as she recognised the back of Brannon's head, wearing a t-shirt, slightly ripped at the neckline, his shoulders rounded.

Oh how the mighty. Annie thought. Maybe not fallen in this case, but certainly a different way to spend a morning than forking out half a million on the idea of a painting. So the woman with him must be the elusive wife. What was wrong with her? Even from the back it was clear she wasn't okay. Too thin, head at an awkward angle, not really looking at the screen.

Swift flicked his fingers, signalling them to close in. They moved quietly, carefully, spreading out around the couple and staying out of view.

"Edward Brannon," Swift said, when they were in place. "You need to come with us. Quietly now."

No response from either of them. The wife completely motionless. Brannon didn't turn towards them, in fact he barely moved, just swinging his head from side to side like a man possessed. Annie exchanged a glance with Tink. Something was wrong. Swift stepped forward, reaching out to grab Brannon from behind and Annie's stomach lurched as she saw a half-used roll of duct tape lying on the arm of the sofa.

"Wait—" she called.

But it was too late. Swift grabbed Brannon's shoulders and wrapped his arm around his neck in a headlock. Annie ran around the sofa, her stomach lurching at what she was faced with. Bile rose in her throat, and she turned, gagging onto the already stained carpet.

"Jesus," Tink called. "Oh god."

Annie felt Tink stumble against her which gave her the literal shove she needed to focus and turn back to the couple. She grabbed at Tink, pulling her close. It wasn't just wrong, it was impossible.

Brannon sat rigid; his body twisted unnaturally within the confines of his bindings. Thick rounds of grey duct tape lashed his wrists together, strapped his arms to his sides, bound his ankles tightly together. His mouth was stretched wide with a stuffed gag, saliva pooling at the corners of his lips, his eyes were bulging with terror.

But it was the woman beside him that turned Annie's blood to ice. Brannon's wife. Margot. The long-lost woman who was at the centre of everything this crime had led them to. Or at least… what was left of her. Her skin was smoothed, mottled green in places, the rest of the colour off, like cheap wax that had been stretched too thinly over her bones. There was a sheen to her that made her look like she'd been dunked in a pot of Modge Podge glue and left to dry. Her eyes were sunken, they would be staring straight ahead without seeing because they weren't eyes, they were marbles. The kind Annie used to play with as a child.

There was no doubt that this woman was dead. But she wasn't just dead, she looked like she had been preserved. Like a specimen in a museum. A sculpture in a gallery. Annie reeled back, thinking of the displays on the plinths around the house outside of this one. The twisted heads. The petrified animals Were they real too?

She'd seen something like this before, a plastination process if she remembered correctly. A *Body Worlds* exhibition years ago, taken when she was still at school. The boys all clinging to each other as they made fun of the naked ladies that Dr Gunther von Hagens had sliced open, frozen in time, forever. Back then it had been a fascinating glimpse of the human body. Now, it was just a horror show.

"What the hell?" Tink's voice barely registered.

Swift let go of Brannon like he'd been burned, stepping back so fast he nearly tripped over the stained carpet. Brannon made a noise—a muffled, strangled cry, his whole body shaking violently as he struggled against his restraints. His wild, panicked eyes darted between them, his face contorting as he tried to speak past the gag. Annie had seen fear before; she'd felt it herself. But this was something else.

Swift recovered fast, running around the sofa and yanking the gag free from Brannon's mouth. The terrified man sucked in air, coughing, spluttering, his throat raw, voice ragged. Annie braced herself. Whatever he was about to say, it was going to be bad.

Brannon's gaze locked onto her, his mouth twisted in terror.

"She—" His voice cracked, hoarse, like he hadn't used it in days. "She's coming."

And then the TV cut out, plummeting the room into silence and darkness so thick Annie couldn't see her hand in front of her face.

"Swift," she hissed.

"I'm here. Tink, you good?"

"No, I'm not bloody good." Tink's voice sounded small. "Has someone taxidermied Margot? Like what the actual f—."

"Clara did it." Brannon's voice echoed through the dark room, making Annie jump. "Get me out of here. She's going to do the same to me. She did the same to your colleague."

"Page?" Tink cried. "No."

"Yes." The voice came from somewhere behind the sofa.

Clara.

The sound of a switch clicking threw them all under a bright, white spotlight. It showed up the utter chaos of the living room. The blood red stains on the threadbare carpet were the lesser of the vulgarities on display. Margot's emaciated body was dressed in a flowery shirt and long skirt. Her embalmed arms like sticks poking out of the sleeves. Brannon had a black eye and a bloody nose, he'd gotten off lightly from the looks of it. And there, standing in the doorway, head tilted, watching them with a smile, was Eliza's young assistant.

"Looks like you finally caught up with me," she said, her voice light, amused. "Took you long enough."

Annie's pulse roared in her ears.

"What have you done with Page?" she shouted.

Clara looked to the yellow stained ceiling. "Oh, my, he's such a cutie. He's going to make a wonderful addition to my collection. I'm not going to display him, though. He's for my own personal use." She cackled and Annie felt sick. "He's so muscly though, the initial prep is taking way too long for my liking. Like, just dry up already."

Clara stepped into the room, in her hands she was swinging a metal baseball bat. Swift pulled himself to his full height, puffing out his chest and placing himself in front of Annie and Tink. They did a dance around the sofa, Clara encroaching on their space, Swift, Tink, and Annie keeping as far away as possible.

"Why?" Swift asked, as Clara rounded the front of the sofa, her eyes falling on the two figures sat there.

Brannon struggled against his restraints.

"Please, love," he said. "Let me go. You and me, we're good."

"Are we really, Dad?" Clara spat. "Because from what I remember, you didn't want me keeping Mr Page, did you?"

"He's a police officer," Brannon shouted. "Of course I tried to stop you. You can't pick a man who will be missed."

"You've got Mum," Clara shouted back, spit flying from her lips. "Why shouldn't I have someone too?"

Mum. So Margot and Brannon had had a daughter. And that daughter was Clara?

"I'm not saying you shouldn't have someone," Brannon tried to placate. "But you need to find someone you love. Who loves you back. Someone who will treat you right."

Clara burst out laughing, dropping her head and waving the bat around above it. In the maelstrom around them, Tink started to slowly edge to the open door. Annie and Swift moved together, trying to hide their DS as she snuck away.

"Treat me right?" Clara spluttered between choked peels. "Like you did mum, you mean? Why do you think I want a non-talking, non-moving doll of a man rather than the man himself? YOU. You're the reason. You knocked the living crap out of mum simply because she looked at another man, or her dress was too short or tight, or her hair looked too groomed, or anything you could use to justify slapping her around the face when you thought no-one was looking. I was looking, Dad. I was looking. And, well now you're making it up to her, aren't you?"

"I am." Brannon sounded frantic. "We're having a lovely time. Your mum is happy. I am happy."

"Good." Clara seemed happy herself with that. "Good, that's okay then."

And Clara was done with her parents for the time being. She directed her gaze towards Annie and Swift, creeping closer, tapping the bat against her open palm.

"Now," she said. "What am I going to do about you two?"

The air seemed to grow thicker as Clara approached. Singed with that same metallic taste that Annie had first smelt back in Eliza's studio. Her head swam, a sudden, sharp pain stabbing behind her eyeballs. Clara cocked her head as Annie staggered backwards, heels of her hands digging into her eyes. As she dragged her hands away, her eyes streaming, she caught sight of a figure behind Clara. It wasn't Brannon or the grotesque mannequin of Margot. This figure swam above the ground, ghostly and ethereal. Female, possibly, though Annie wasn't sure because each time she blinked the shadow of her body moved.

Somewhere beside her she heard Swift calling out, asking if she was okay, but he sounded like he was underwater. Or maybe it was Annie who was drowning. Her throat scratched and her lungs burnt like they were full of water.

The figure slid across the living room straight towards Annie and as it got closer, she saw the face from the unfinished portrait, mouth stretched wide in a toothless grin. Her bladder loosened and her legs felt like jelly.

"Getaway," she screamed, lifting her arms and covering her head. "Get away from me."

But shouting made no difference as the ghost-like shadow descended.

TWENTY-THREE

Annie's scream bounced off the walls like shrapnel. Yet the ghost kept coming, her mouth stretched wide, a cavernous howl of silence. Not a sound passed her lips, but the air screamed anyway. A pressure building in Annie's chest, rattling her ribs like the warning toll of a bell.

She stumbled backwards, hands flailing, ready to strike at something that might not even be real. Her heel hit the toe of Swift's boot, and she went down hard, her shoulder thudding into the door frame behind her.

The shadow loomed over her. Closer now. Annie's breath snagged in her throat, pain blooming across her back.

"Annie." Swift's voice cracked the fog.

Somewhere beyond the figure, Clara let out a screech of laughter.

Annie blinked once. Twice. And the ghost's face

shifted again. This time it wasn't malevolent. Not a threat anymore. It looked mournful. She wasn't here to hurt Annie. She was here to help. The shadow's translucent arm lifted, fingers splayed, and it pointed. Annie followed the hand to the darkness under the sofa. Something was wedged there; a glint of silver catching the harsh overhead light. It was a knife.

Her fingers scrambled over the grimy carpet, heart hammering, until she wrapped her hand around the handle. It was small, a kitchen blade, streaked with something dark she didn't want to think about, and with a surge of adrenaline, Annie scrambled to her feet and turned. Clara was advancing on them both, the rusted metal bat swinging lazily in her grip. Her eyes were wild, her mouth twitching in a grin that looked sewn on.

"No," Annie growled, and she ran faster than she'd ever moved in her life, straight at Clara, the small knife gripped tightly in her hands.

Clara noticed just in time to step to the side to avoid the blade, the full weight of Annie knocked her off balance, both of them tumbling to the floor in a tangle of limbs. The knife buckled against the bat—twisting Annie's wrist back on itself with a pop of ligaments and pain—and clattered across the carpet. But Annie didn't need it anymore. She had Clara and a heartful of rage.

Clara screamed. A bloodcurdling, furious scream. "You stupid, stupid—."

Swift was already moving. He dropped to his

knees, catching Clara's wrists just as she started thrashing beneath Annie.

"I've got her arms." Swift had all his body weight on the woman.

"Her legs," Annie barked, breathless.

Clara bucked again, nearly throwing them both off.

Swift looked around. "The tape. Grab the tape!"

Brannon was moaning behind them, still bound, tears streaking his bloodied face. Annie reached past his shuddering body and snatched the half-used roll of duct tape from where it had fallen from the arm of the sofa.

"I've got it—hold her," Annie called, tearing the end of the tape with her teeth.

"I am holding her."

"Harder!"

They fought like animals, Clara flailing and snapping, teeth bared, eyes wild with something far beyond fury. But Annie had adrenaline, and Swift had bulk. Between the two of them, they pinned her down long enough for Annie to wrap the tape around her wrists—once, twice, three times—binding them tightly by her chest.

"Legs," Swift grunted, and Annie scrambled down, rolling the tape over Clara's ankles like she was mummifying her.

"Is it tight?"

"Tight enough," Annie cried, dropping to the floor, heaving in great lungfuls of rotten air. "My head, Swift. It feels like it's going to burst. Did you see it? Did you see the ghost?"

Annie dragged herself to standing; Swift caught her arm and helped her up and they looked down at their catch who was writhing like a landed fish, grin still firmly on her face.

"Oh yes," she said, giggling like a child. "I sometimes forget the effect of the Pyrethroid on other people. Seeing things, are we? Hearing voices?"

Clara laughed again, spit drooling from her lips as she tried to sit herself up. Neither Annie nor Swift moved to help her. Annie ached all over, her head was cracking open, but even if she'd been at her fittest, she still wouldn't have moved an inch.

"Don't think I didn't see your colleague leave," Clara went on. "I'm not stupid. If she's going in search of Tom then she'll succumb to it too. She'll be overcome with a madness that has been known to make people throw themselves in front of trains."

Swift stuck his head out the door and started to call for Tink. Footsteps thundered from somewhere nearby, the unmistakable weight of uniformed boots, radios crackling. Back-up was finally here.

Clara only laughed, even as the sound drew nearer. Still bound, still grinning, blood crusting at the corner of her mouth where her face had smacked against the floor.

"Too late," she sing-songed, head lolling like a rag doll. "The poison's already done its job. Don't worry, it'll wear off soon enough. Maybe. I never really know how it's going to work, except that it only affects women, weird, right?"

Annie stood over her, breath shallow. The metallic taste still coated her mouth, her limbs shaking from adrenaline and whatever it was that was lacing the air. But this wasn't over. She needed Clara to talk before she was swept away in cuffs.

"Tell me what happened to Eliza," Annie said, her voice low and firm. "Tell me why you killed her."

Clara's eyes snapped to hers, the laughter momentarily slipping. Something had changed in her, the mask cracking a little.

"You really want the truth?" she asked, blinking like a child who'd been caught scribbling on the walls. "Or do you want the version that makes sense on paper? That Eliza felt sorry for poor mum-less me and hired me as her assistant as soon as I finished school? Guilt, more like."

"I want to know why Eliza Warren ended up dead in her own studio," Annie snapped. "Tell me what she did to deserve that."

"She watched." Clara's grin shrank. Her voice dropped to a whisper. "She watched and she said nothing. She painted it instead."

Swift stood frozen beside her. The footsteps were getting louder now — someone shouted down the corridor, but neither of them looked away from Clara.

"She was friends with Mum, you know. Eliza and Margot. Painted each other's portraits. Eliza called Mum her muse." Clara spat the last word like it had burned her tongue. "But then Brannon came along. Mr Golden Touch. And she stood by while he broke my mother's face."

Annie's heart thudded in her chest.

"You were there?"

Clara nodded, the slightest movement. "I was a child. I had no idea anything was wrong between my parents. But Eliza? She could've saved her. She could've *said* something. She could have told them about my dad when Mum went missing."

"And the painting?" Swift asked.

Clara smiled again, slow and bitter. "That bloody painting. I knew nothing about it for years. Eliza must have kept it hidden in her bedroom. It showed Mum's bruises, so Eliza must have known what *he* was doing to her. But she never took it to the police. Never warned anyone. It was just a study to her. Just *art*."

The sound of radios crackled closer. Clara turned her head to listen, but she kept talking.

"I had no idea she even had that painting until I saw it in her studio, returned by Vivienne because she'd accidentally picked it up for the exhibition."

"You realised it was your mum," Annie whispered.

Clara nodded again. "And I realised that Eliza had known all along. She'd known what he did to her. And she did *nothing*."

"And Vivienne?" Swift asked sharply.

Clara's eyes flashed. "Vivienne saw the painting during the exhibition set-up. She vaguely recognised

Margot too, from the news stories that had been around at the time. That's when she started poking around — started blackmailing Dad, threatening Eliza. Said she'd go to the press with it. Said she wanted money or she'd go to the police. Said the world would know what Eliza had covered up. And what Dad had done. I think she wanted to be famous.

And then when Vivienne started to lead you to the truth, I knew she had to die. She sent you cryptic messages, because she didn't want to get her hands dirty either. Coward."

"That was Vivienne?" Annie felt relief that she hadn't imagined the disappearing message. It was brief, there was still more to learn. "Did Eliza tell you what happened to your mum? Did she know?"

Clara tilted her head. "No. She begged me not to say anything. She didn't know I already knew. She just… she cracked. She told me she remembered Mum turning up at her door with blood on her face. And she *still* did nothing. So, I gave her a choice." Her grin returned, wide and toothy. "Live with it or die with it."

"You poisoned her," Annie said softly.

"I laced the paint," Clara replied. "It's a rare compound. Absorbs through the skin. Causes hallucinations, paranoia, confusion. I gave her just enough to make her see Margot again. Made her believe the painting was *alive*. Talking to her. Judging her." She laughed. "And then… I waited."

Swift swore under his breath.

"You made her think she was losing her mind," Annie said.

"She was," Clara whispered. "But not fast enough. So I helped. A little push. A nudge one night in her studio. With help, of course. I took Mum with me. You should have seen Eliza's face. She was so funny, clawing away at Mum like she was the one who would hurt her."

Clara burst out laughing, the sound making Annie's legs wobble.

"Jesus," Swift muttered.

"They all deserved it," Clara went on, eyes shining now, almost dreamy. "They buried the truth for decades. But I didn't. I *dug it up*. Literally."

Annie felt her stomach twist. "What do you mean?"

Clara nodded. "When I was old enough, after Mum disappeared, Dad told me that she had run off. Said she was selfish. I believed him for years. But I put two and two together years ago, because I'd seen Dad's temper first hand. I knew Dad must have killed her." Her voice dropped to a whisper. "He didn't even bury her properly. He confessed all to me one night when he'd had too much vodka to drink. Laced vodka, obviously. Told me Mum was stuffed into a freezer in the old warehouse where she disappeared. He'd gotten angry because she was looking at men all night. Pushed her hard enough to bash her head in.

You lot didn't look very thoroughly, did you? The warehouse may have changed into flats, but the basement stayed the same. The freezer wasn't even that well hidden. A grave for Mum. Only I wanted her back. So, I brought her home. Here."

The backup burst into the corridor. Shouts, movement, the slam of boots. Clara didn't flinch. She sat in her bindings like a queen on her throne, eyes wide and fixed on Annie.

"Kept her for myself, didn't I?" Clara said. "I had to do a bit of research into how, but you can find anything on the internet these days. Dad even built me this little home so I could have somewhere to keep my practice people. I could have happily stayed here, making sure Dad paid for what he did, if it hadn't been for Eliza and her stupid bloody portrait. Dad tried to buy it, so no-one else could see it, but he failed. Just like he did in everything he tries. I wasn't having you lot take Mum away from me, not again."

Officers poured into the room. Someone gasped behind Annie. The plastinated body. Brannon's bruises. Clara's grin. Swift stepped away from Annie, intercepting the team.

"Secure the scene. We need medics and a full forensics team down here now."

Clara didn't resist as they lifted her, duct-taped and dazed, from the carpet. As she passed Annie, she whispered: "You saw her too, didn't you? In the painting. She's not finished with you either."

Annie's spine locked, but she didn't answer. She couldn't. Because deep in her chest, something cold had settled. Something that made her think Clara might not be entirely wrong.

Annie stood frozen as Clara was carried out, the echo of her final words still ringing in her ears. *You saw her too, didn't you?* Her eyes burned. Her head pounded. The world tilted, just slightly, as if everything she thought was solid had softened at the edges.

Swift touched her arm, grounding her. "You okay?"

"No," Annie replied, scrunching her face. "But I'm still standing. Just. You?"

Before Swift could say more, a shout came from the hallway.

"Swift." It was Tink. Her voice was high and panicked. "Swift. Annie. You need to get here right now."

Annie didn't wait. She ran, slipping past the officers crowding the corridor, following the sound of Tink's boots hammering down the passage and around a corner into a narrow, windowless hallway. Tink was already crouched beside a closed door at the far end, her face white as bone, peering into the keyhole.

"I found him," she whispered, not looking at them. "But… I think we're too late. I can't get in."

Annie's heart dropped. She moved past Tink's sobbing outline, bracing herself as Swift shoulder barged the door open, splintered wood flying everywhere. Inside, the room was bright as strip lights buzzed overhead. A plastic sheet covered the floor, the table at the centre was stainless steel. A tray of gleaming tools sat beside it. And on the table, utterly still, was Page.

He was shirtless, pale, arms resting at his sides. There were tubes taped to his veins, trailing to stands with unknown bags of fluid hanging from them. A cannula in the crook of his elbow. His face was slack, head tilted away, mouth slightly open.

"No," Annie breathed, her knees nearly buckling as she ran forward and tugged the needles from his arms. "No, no, no. Page, you're safe now. We're here."

Tink hovered just inside the door, one hand pressed to her mouth.

"Is he…" she whispered. "What has she done to him?"

Annie placed her fingers on Page's neck. "Please," she muttered. "Please don't be dead."

A flutter. So faint she thought she imagined it but there it was again.

She snapped her head toward Swift. "He's alive. Get a medical team in here right now."

Swift turned and bellowed down the corridor. Annie gripped Page's wrist now, desperate to feel something more. His skin was clammy, the colour all wrong, but there was a pulse. She wasn't imagining it. Tink ran into the room and wrapped her arms around Page's bare chest.

"We've got you," Tink whispered. "Hang in there, Page. You stubborn, beautiful bastard."

Footsteps thundered down the hallway. Then paramedics were there, pushing past, assessing, speaking in clipped, sharp commands. Annie and Tink stepped back, out of their way to let them get to work.

Page was alive. They hadn't lost him. But as she looked at the metal tray of tools beside the table, she knew how close it had been and how much of a difficult journey Page still had to fight. Seconds later and Clara would've finished her masterpiece.

"Come on," Swift said quietly. "Page is in good hands. Let's get out of this house of horrors.

TWENTY-FOUR
TWO WEEKS LATER

The grass was damp but spring-warm, speckled with buttercups and a sprinkling of fallen cherry blossom. A gentle breeze stirred the trees, carrying with it the scent of freshly turned soil. The mourners were walking away, comforting each other in their suits of black and navy. They would be off to eat sandwiches and drink tea and talk about the memories they shared of the dead.

Annie stood with her arms folded across her chest, the wind nudging her coat open, her hair dancing across her cheeks. She wasn't crying—she thought she might—but instead there was only a heavy calm, like the moment just after a thunderstorm, when the air still crackled with what had passed.

The headstone was a simple grey marble with clean lines, unpretentious. Just her name and a small epitaph.

. . .

Margot Grayson. Beloved friend and sister

The MCU stood quietly, waiting for the crowds to disperse before they paid their own respects. They didn't often go to the funerals of the victims on their cases, but Margot's had felt different. She had waited for twenty years to be properly laid to rest, and Annie wanted to make sure it happened. Swift stood beside her, his arm gently looped though hers. Tink was a step behind, her hand resting lightly on Page's wheelchair. He looked pale, the bandages were mostly gone now, but his body was still suffering from the effects of being pumped with fluids designed to kill off live tissues ready for plastination. Luckily, Clara had made her own concoction from drugs readily available on the internet, so they hadn't been as potent as they might have been.

Dominic Grayson stepped forward from where he'd been standing beside his sister's grave. He looked thinner, the grief of decades etched deep in his features, but there was peace in him now, too. He held out a hand, shaking Swift's, then Annie's.

"You brought her home," he said, voice low. "You gave her back to me."

Annie nodded. "I'm so sorry for your loss, Mr Grayson. Only hope that today can help you grieve properly now you know the truth."

He looked over at the headstone. "I will, thank

you. Though the truth is hard to swallow, at least I know Margot is safe now."

They all stood there for a moment longer, heads bowed.

"I used to call her Magpie," Dominic continued, softly, his voice raw. "She hated it. Said it made her sound like a scavenger." He let out a laugh. "But she always kept things. Notes, photos, old ticket stubs. Like she was afraid that if she threw anything away, she'd lose the memory of it too."

Annie swallowed hard, her throat tight.

Dominic walked to the headstone and let his hand settle gently against the marble, his touch so soft it was almost reverent. "I spent years hoping she was out there. That she had gotten away. That maybe…" His voice caught, and he shook his head. "But I think I always knew, deep down. I just didn't want to admit it."

Annie exhaled softly. "You never stopped looking for her."

Dominic's lips pressed into a thin line. "No. But I stopped hoping. And I hate myself for that."

Annie's chest ached. She had seen it before; grief wrapped in guilt; regret tangled with loss. It didn't matter that Dominic had done everything he could. He would always feel like it wasn't enough.

"This wasn't your fault," Swift said.

Dominic let out a slow breath, his fingers curling into a fist against the headstone. "Yeah?" His voice was bitter. "Then why does it feel like it is?"

Annie stepped forward. "Because you loved her. And you wanted the best for her."

Dominic closed his eyes for a moment. Then, finally, he nodded. For a long time, none of them spoke. Dominic's hand lingered for another second before he finally pulled back. His shoulders were rigid, his face a careful mask of control, but when he turned away, Annie saw the tears brimming in his eyes.

"She was just a kid," he murmured, shaking his head. "She deserved so much more than this."

Annie felt a lump rise in her throat. "Yeah. She did."

Dominic swallowed hard, pressing his lips together. "She always wanted to be remembered." His gaze flickered back to the grave. "And, at least now, she will be."

He took a slow step back, his body heavy with grief, but something in his posture shifted. Like a weight had finally settled instead of floating in limbo. He could finally mourn her the way he was supposed to. He turned towards the team, his voice stronger this time. "Make sure Brannon doesn't walk away from this."

"He won't," Swift said. "I promise you he is going to go away for a long time. They both are."

Dominic nodded. "Good."

Then, with one last look at his sister's grave, he turned and walked away, leaving the four members of the MCU alone with the dead.

"Back to yours?" Tink asked after a beat, trying to steer Page across the grass with one hand, the other holding her coat closed against the breeze. It wasn't going well and his wheels edged precariously close to a freshly dug, empty grave.

"Tink," Page called. "Not yet, yeah. I think we have established that I'm hanging around for a little while longer."

Tink laughed and grabbed the chair with both hands, throwing her coat over his shoulders so she could steer properly.

"Nice try though," Page added, laughing.

"There is a suspicious quantity of unopened supermarket Prosecco waiting at mine," Swift said, answering Tink's question. "So yes, let's all meet back there."

"Luxury," Page muttered.

"And we're having that Easter egg hunt if it kills us," Tink added, pushing Page's chair alongside her yellow Punto as they all helped him into the passenger seat.

"I think the egg sandwiches probably would kill you if you ate them now," Annie joked, linking her arm through Swift's.

"I threw those out days ago." Swift unlocked the car. "They made my kitchen smell like the station toilets."

"Nice." Page did up his belt. "That's my appetite gone."

"Nope," Tink called as she climbed in. "You're on

a strict diet of as many calories as we can feed you. And I want my easter egg hunt. I swear if a badger's eaten my Lindt balls, someone's paying the price."

"Probably the badger," Page muttered as he pulled his door shut.

They arrived at Swift's house just as the sun broke properly through the clouds, flooding the garden in a stunning golden hue. The egg trail markers were still tucked beneath bushes and wound around tree trunks. A few of the foil-wrapped prizes had vanished, pecked at or gnawed away, but many had survived, tucked behind planters and buried in grass. The garden still looked wild, but it was perfect for the occasion.

Tink helped Page down onto a picnic blanket with exaggerated care, then immediately pelted him with a Cadbury Mini Egg as soon as he was seated.

"Ow, don't hit a man while he's down." He grabbed the eggs as Tink threw them and shoved them into his mouth.

Swift went inside and returned with drinks, a plate of freshly made cheese sandwiches, and a very crushed Victoria sponge. "Don't judge me. It's been in the fridge since Sunday."

Annie stretched out on the grass beside him, one shoe kicked off, her eyes closed to the sun. The world felt warm again. Safe, for the first time in days.

"So," she said lazily, "do we think the ghost was real?"

Tink scoffed. "No. Gaslighting and chemicals, remember?"

Annie raised a brow. "I dunno. Something showed me where to find that knife. We might not be here if she hadn't."

"You probably saw it when we walked in the room," Swift said, taking a swig of lemonade. "Your poisoned subconscious popped out to remind you when you needed it most."

They all laughed. Even Annie. It was a little cracked, a little tired, but it was real.

She didn't feel haunted by the case, or the past, or the echoes of things left unsaid. Because Margot had a grave now and Clara and Brannon were in custody and would be spending the rest of their lives behind bars.

The unfinished painting was locked in evidence storage, trapped away for the rest of its life. Along with all the paintings Brannon had kept, including every painting Eliza had ever done of Margot—an obsession that didn't end with her death. It made sense that he didn't want anyone else getting his hands on the one that gave away his secret.

The forensic team were working through the sculptures Clara had made, documenting each grotesque piece with grim precision. Every bust, every limb, every horrifically warped face; evidence that she'd been practising, perfecting, long before she turned her skills on her own mother. Some of them were animals. But not all of them. And not enough of them.

Annie stared at the sky for a long moment, the brightness of it jarring. The warmth on her skin didn't match the cold still shifting somewhere under her ribs. The rest of MCU were scattered across the grass behind Swift's house, a loose, quiet group. Eating crushed cake, trading sarcastic comments and stretching out sore muscles and stolen hours of peace. It was rare, this. To come out of something so awful intact.

"You know," Tink said, tearing the foil from a slightly soggy chocolate bunny, "Something good came from this case."

"Elaborate," Swift said, grabbing a sandwich from the tray.

"I've got a date tomorrow night with a certain Ben Harebell." Tink popped a Mini Egg in her mouth and her cheeks flushed a pastel pink much the same colour.

"No way!" Annie sat upright. "The auctioneer?"

"Yep."

"His name's Harebell?" Page laughed.

"What of it?" Tink threw Page a look.

"Oh, nothing," Page grinned. "Just, you know, if you guys end up getting married, your name with be Tink Harebell. Tinkerbell. Ha."

"Oh god," Tink dropped onto her back, her hands

covering her face as her team burst into laughter around her.

Annie glanced at her, then at Page, then let her gaze drift to the garden, real life creeping back in at the edges. She loved her team. A flicker of movement caught her eye, just beyond the willow tree. A shape. A shift. A suggestion of something watching. She blinked and it was gone. Tink caught her looking and glanced over her shoulder.

"Annie," Tink said, smiling. "If that's a ghost you've just seen, tell her to point me in the direction of the rest of the hidden eggs. I could use all the sugar I can get my hands on."

And as the MCU burst again into fits of giggles around her, Annie lifted a hand in thanks to the memory of Margot who was showing her the way to a large box of Creme Eggs poking out between the dangling willow branches, halfway up the tree.

Thank you so much for reading **The Ghost Portrai**t.

If you would like to join O'Malley & Swift on their next adventure, you can find out more below.

ESCAPE ROOM

It was meant to be fun. Now they're dying to leave.

O'Malley and Swift join the rest of the MCU for what's supposed to be a well-earned break from the chaos of their day jobs. A luxury Escape Room. When Evans turns up last minute to complete the group, they know they've got the winning team.

But the moment the doors lock behind them, things start to feel off.

The puzzles are cruel. The tasks are twisted. And the "game" doesn't end when the timer hits zero.

Someone has built a house of horrors—designed to maim, torture, and kill. And he's not going to stop until he's had his fun.

He wanted victims. He got O'Malley and Swift.

Can they solve the clues before the Escape Room claims its next victim?

Order now
KTGallowaybooks.com

THANK YOU!

Thank you so much for reading THE GHOST PORTRAIT. It's hard for me to put into words how much I appreciate my readers. You're all amazing.

If you enjoyed THE GHOST PORTRAIT, I would greatly appreciate it if you took the time to review on your favourite platforms.

You can also find me at www.KTGallowaybooks.com

ALSO BY K.T. GALLOWAY

The O'Malley & Swift adventures available to buy now!

CORN DOLLS

Their first case sees Annie and Joe on the hunt for a young girl who is missing. Snatched from her home during a game of hide and seek. Left behind in her place is a doll crudely twisted from stalks of corn.

FOXTON GIRLS

When a spate of suicides occur at prestigious girls' school, Foxton's, Psychotherapist Annie O'Malley is called in to talk with the students.

What Annie finds are troubled young girls full of secrets and lies; and a teacher caught in the midst.

WE ALL FALL DOWN

When a young woman falls ill and dies after a night out, her friends blame a cloaked figure that had been stalking them in the streets. A masked face with hooked beak, immediately recognisable as a Plague Doctor.

THE HOUSE OF SECRETS

With a lead on her missing sister, Annie and Joe travel north and rent a small cottage in the village where Mim was last spotted. Only, the village has a dark history of its own. The cottage was home to a family who haven't been seen in over forty years. Their things still packed away in the basement, awaiting their return. It's a macabre destination for the dark tourist, and the rest of the village isn't much more welcoming.

THE UNINVITED GUEST

Back in Norfolk and back to work, Annie O'Malley and DI Swift are called to an isolated seaside village and the exclusive Paradise Grove Spa. Renowned for its peace and tranquility, the spa and its staff offer the chance to relax and recuperate in a discrete private setting on its own causeway. So when a dead body turns up in one of the rooms with no clue to who he is or how he got there, suspicion falls on the secretive group of guests.

DEADLY GAMES

When Annie and Joe are called to the local park to investigate reports of vandalism, they begin one of the most harrowing cases of their career. The vandal is a scared young woman with a bomb strapped to her chest and a list of games she must play. As the games get more gruesome, the young woman has a choice to make; kill or be killed.

ONE LAST BREATH

After the distress of Annie O'Malley's last case, she's in need of a bit of rest and recuperation. So her sister, Mim, books them on a flight to a luxury all inclusive resort in Spain for a break. But what was supposed to be a chance to sip sangria and reconnect with each other after so long apart soon turns into something terrifying when a group of armed men storm the hotel and take the guests hostage.

VANISHING ACT

When the celebrated illusionist, Gabriel Mirage, is found dead in the midst of his own vanishing act, O'Malley and Swift are thrust into a realm where the truth is as elusive as the disappearing act itself.

CHILL PILL

Annie finally reconnects with her father, only for him to be arrested and beaten to a coma. Can she and Swift clear his name so Annie can find out the truth of her childhood before it's too late?

BLEEDING HEARTS

In the game of love, losing your heart can be deadly. When six bodies are found in an abandoned pool, hearts missing, O'Malley and Swift race to stop a killer with a twisted message. Can they unravel the truth before another heart is stolen

THE GHOST PORTRAIT

When renowned artist, Eliza Warren, prepares her final exhibition, one portrait refuses to stay silent. The unfinished painting of a woman shifts, her face twisting with a sinister life of its own. As shadows close in, Eliza realises her masterpiece isn't just art—it's a deadly secret waiting to be unleashed.

ESCAPE ROOM

O'Malley, Swift, and the MCU Team head off to a well-deserved away day in a luxury escape room. But the moment the doors are locked behind them, things start to feel off. The puzzles are cruel, the tasks are twisted, and the game doesn't end when the timer hits zero.

Printed in Dunstable, United Kingdom